THE GARDEN

MEGHAN FERRARI

Red Deer Press

Published in Canada by Red Deer Press
195 Allstate Parkway, Markham, ON   L3R 4T8

Published in the United States by Red Deer Press
311 Washington Street, Brighton, MA   02135

Library and Archives Canada Cataloguing in Publication
Ferrari, Meghan, author
The garden / Meghan Ferrari.

ISBN 978-0-88995-568-4 (softcover)

I. Title.

PS8611.E766G37 2018   jC813'.6   C2018-904631-7

Publisher Cataloging-in-Publication Data (U.S.)
Names: Ferrari, Meghan, author.
Title: The Garden / Meghan Ferrari.
Description: Markham, Ontario : Red Deer Press, 2018. | Summary: "In the middle of an
international conflict between the Syrian Army and Rebels, and after witnessing the tragedy of war
and the indignities of a refugee camp, Elias finds himself an immigrant in North America where he
comes face to face with culture shock, racism, and bullying" – Provided by publisher.

Identifiers: ISBN 978-0-88995-568-4 (paperback)
Subjects: LCSH: Refugee camps – Syria -- Fiction. | Racism – Fiction. | Bullying – Fiction. |
BISAC: YOUNG ADULT FICTION / Social Themes / Emigration & Immigration. | YOUNG
ADULT FICTION / People & Places / Middle East.
Classification: LCC PZ7.1F477Ga | DDC 813.6 – dc23

Design by Tanya Montini
Edited for the press by Peter Carver
Printed in Canada by Copywell

ONTARIO ARTS COUNCIL
CONSEIL DES ARTS DE L'ONTARIO
an Ontario government agency
un organisme du gouvernement de l'Ontario

Canada Council   Conseil des arts
for the Arts   du Canada

Red Deer Press acknowledges with thanks the Canada Council for the Arts
and the Ontario Arts Council for their support of our publishing program.
We acknowledge the financial support of the Government of Canada through
the Canada Book Fund (CBF) for our publishing activities.

www.reddeerpress.com

For our newcomers

CHAPTER 1

SYRIA

It sounds like heavy rain, the dirt being tossed on the sheet of plywood inches above our heads.

My brother and I sit below, in the hole my mother dug for us in her garden. There is not enough room for us to stretch our legs, so we keep them hugged tightly to our chests.

This is our third time underground.

I sense Moussa's little hand on my thigh before I feel its clamminess clutching my fingers. I give his hand a quick squeeze and then open it, as Mama did when we were young. With my index finger, I begin to trace light circles on his palm. As I'd hoped, this makes him giggle uncontrollably, but I shush him to be quiet.

The rebels are walking the streets.

Packs of armed men, clad in checkered keffiyehs worn like bandanas, are looking for children, their most coveted weapons— to train, to arm, and to thrust into battle.

To be a child in Syria is fatal.

"Elias?"

"Yes, Moussa?"

"Where did Baba find our roof?"

"In the alley, on his way home from the clinic."

"And he carried it home so we could play?"

"Yes, Moussa, so we could play," I reply, pretending for his sake that the terror of hiding for our lives is just a game.

I think back to that night months ago, when the shelling in the neighboring village had kept me awake, and I'd heard our father and mother arguing in the kitchen.

"I won't bring our sons to that shelter anymore!"

I heard the scraping of Baba's chair as he rose quickly to his feet.

"There's no electricity, no food—only fear! What kind of place is that for children?"

"It's our only chance of survival!" Mama shouted. "You tell me what options we have. Who's coming to help us, Peter? No one! The world has turned its back on us."

"I haven't turned mine, Lena! I'd die first."

The door slammed, and when I awoke later that night and looked through my bedroom window, I saw the silver light of the moon glinting off the garden shovel in my mother's hand and the weathered piece of plywood at my father's side.

"What are we today?" Moussa asks.

Last time, Moussa and I were rats who had to hunt for food and hide from the traps above.

And the time before, we were playing hide and seek. Hours later, when the hiding spot had begun to feel like a grave, Baba and Mama crept out of the house and gently lifted the sheet of wood. Moussa had fallen asleep, his chestnut hair matted to his forehead.

Baba reached down and scooped him up into his thick arms.

"You found me," Moussa murmured, sleepily.

And Baba wept.

That night when we were snuggled in our beds, I told Moussa it was because Baba was so happy—he had never before won a game of hide and seek with us.

"Today, Moussa, we are your favorite flower."

"The jasmine!"

"Yes, Syria's strong and sweet jasmine." I pretend to sniff him and he giggles. "And we are its seeds being planted."

Moussa wiggles as though trying to root himself deeper in the earth, and I chuckle.

"And one day," I continue, struggling to stay upbeat, "when we see the sun shine again … we will grow, blossom, and bring happiness to others."

I can sense that Moussa is smiling, but I do not join him.

Because right now, there is no sunshine in Syria.

Only darkness.

CHAPTER 2

CANADA

"Good work, bud," Mr. Connolly says, dropping Elias's functions quiz onto his desk and continuing to the front of the classroom.

"Nicely done, Hussein!" Joshua mimics Connolly's enthusiastic tone, snatching the test from Elias's hands.

"Give it here!" Ben, Josh's sidekick, swipes it from his fingers.

"Ninety-six! Wow, way to go, Muhammad! Another four percent and you'll be building those bombs!"

"Boom!" Joshua and Ben exclaim, fist bumping.

"Now all you gotta do is work on that beard, baby face." Josh goes to caress Elias's chin but Elias smacks his hand away.

"Whoa! Careful, J, you're pressing his button ... his detonation button!"

"Bah-zing!" Laughing, the boys high five and lean back in their chairs.

"Whatever, dumb and dumber. At least Elias doesn't have to use his fingers when he counts." Sitting diagonally across from Elias, Liling grabs the quiz from Ben's hands and, with a flick of her delicate wrist, shoots it back to Elias's desk.

"You're right, Liling," Josh replies. "Watch me count. One," he says, giving her the middle finger.

Josh and Ben burst into laughter.

Ignoring the boys, Liling tucks a rogue strand of black hair behind her ear and smiles sympathetically at Elias.

Elias does not meet her eye, but continues to stare at the quiz before him, until the words begin to blur and the numbers—the only things that still make sense to him—begin to lose their meaning.

The bell rings and Elias makes his way through the crowded halls to the cafeteria.

He grabs a chair at his usual empty table by the window, overlooking the high school's football field. *Soccer field*, he corrects himself with a sigh, remembering that's what Canadians call the game.

He settles in and watches the line that has begun to snake out from the lunch counter—a steady stream of kids entering empty-handed and exiting with trays teetering with food.

Over the past month in Canada, Elias has come to regard cafeteria food as tragic—not because of its taste (he'd been warned about that)—but because it often ends up thrown around or tossed out.

Dismayed, he pulls a bruised pear and a small container of last night's kibbeh from his knapsack and sets them on the table before him.

He turns toward the window, then lowers his gaze to avoid the reflection of his own eyes, focusing instead on the field below, where red leaves are beginning to cover the green.

He stares out, remembering the smell of freshly cut grass beneath his feet, the feel of sweat on his brow, and the blue of the cloudless sky, as Rafi chanted his name and his soccer ball soared through peeling yellow posts.

"Elias? Earth to Elias." A voice calls him back to the cafeteria and he looks up to see Liling and a short boy with unruly red hair staring down at him.

"Can we join you?" Liling asks. She sets down her tray and swings her legs easily over the bench.

"This is Sullivan." Liling gestures to the boy who has climbed in clumsily beside her. "We run the Art Club together."

The redhead gives a small salute before pulling out his phone, turning it sideways, and tapping his thumbs rapidly on the screen.

Elias nods and redirects his attention to the bulgur and lamb before him. He can feel the anger rising within him.

He hadn't asked them to join him. He hadn't said they could.

He didn't want to make friends. He didn't need to.

He is going back.

He is going to rebuild his country.

These relationships in his Canadian school are short lived. Like the small carton of chocolate milk on Liling's tray, they come with an expiration date.

"It's Arts Week this week," Liling says. She's pointing to the giant paint-by-number banner of the Canadian wilderness that the club had tacked on the wall opposite the lunch counter earlier that morning. "Kind of cool, all these kids coming together with different colors to complete this picture."

Elias nods and shovels a large spoonful of bulgur into his mouth—enough to prevent him from having to reply.

"Tomorrow, a makeup artist will be here, turning students into zombies." Liling grins.

Elias eyes the crowd of students staring into their screens and thinks it won't be too hard to make them brainless.

He settles his eyes on Sullivan, who has not looked up from his phone since he sat down. Elias has come to feel that despite having information literally in the palms of their hands, the majority of these students have not heard of the civil war in Syria. Unlike him, they have no knowledge of the Syrian Army, the Rebels, or Daesh—or the conflict that has been raging for years. Elias bets that they couldn't even pinpoint his country on a map. And he knows with great certainty that each time they refresh their Facebook page, a new eulogy for a dead Syrian does not appear.

Turning back to the window, Elias wonders about the world's growing fascination with zombies. They're everywhere: books, movies, television. He doesn't understand why zombies scare people. They don't frighten him in the least. Elias knows from his own experience that it isn't the dead you have to fear. It's the living.

"Do you play soccer?" Liling inquires.

"No," Elias replies, then looks away from the field.

The thought is too painful.

He packs up his lunch, picks up his knapsack, and makes his way toward the red Exit sign. It's a beacon that has been beckoning him all lunch-hour long.

CHAPTER 3

SYRIA

School is closed today.

Our teachers are worried about missiles and the fact that there is not enough room for us all in the underground classroom.

Last week, my father had Youssef, his best friend from medical school, over for dinner. Long after Moussa had gone to bed, and while I was in my room reading, I heard Youssef telling Baba about a mortar shell that had struck an elementary school near his hospital in Damascus.

"I have never seen anything like it, Peter." He paused, and I heard the bottle of wine being set back on the table.

"Five children and three teachers. When they brought them in ..." I heard him struggling to find the words "... their injuries were so great ..."

"I'm sorry, Youssef." I imagined Baba placing a hand on top of his friend's.

"Students and teachers, Peter. Education is the reweaving of society's fabric. What will happen when there is no one left to weave ... or worse yet, when there is no fabric?"

I put my book down as I felt the rage, like a stoked fire, burning in my chest.

I thought of the small room beneath the school—dark, dank, and dreary—the space originally meant to house the janitor's supplies.

It is a place for decay.

Not for the future.

Moussa and I sit at the kitchen table.

I am working on rational numbers and he is drawing a picture with an inky black marker.

"Is that another one for the fridge, Moussa?"

His brown curls bounce as he bobs his head up and down.

I look over my shoulder to where our mother has taped his drawings, like pieces of a quilt, to the refrigerator door.

Simple shapes depict our town's rocky land and rugged mountains. Vibrant colors show Baba in front of his medical clinic and Mama beside her hyacinths. The one in the center is of the two of us, my arm snug around my brother's shoulders.

There is a sharp knock at the door.

Collectively, we inhale.

"Wait here." Baba holds a firm hand in the air.

He reaches for the brass handle, hesitates, and then opens the door a crack, letting a slit of light in.

Baba's body relaxes.

"Hello, little friend," he says and opens the door wide to

reveal our neighbor's son. He's framed in sunshine, a muddy football in hand.

"Rafi!" I break into a smile as Baba leads him in.

"Elias, please tell me you're not doing homework when school is closed!"

He drops onto the seat beside me and removes the pencil from my hand.

"The weather is twenty-five degrees today, and there is no Mrs. Beshur to call us back in."

"Call us? She has to chase you back inside!"

"It is good for her figure." We laugh, as Mama's hand goes to her hip and Baba holds back a smile.

"C'mon, Elias. The field is open and the sky is our own." Rafi gestures to the window, to the cloudless blue of the day.

He begins to tug on the delicate silver cross around his neck that his grandmother gave him for his confirmation last year, and I know that he is anxious. Baba, being a doctor, says that life pours out of Rafi like a pierced artery; he cannot sit still.

"Baba, may I go play football with Rafi?"

"No, son. Not today."

"But, Baba, we don't have school, and I've almost finished the next lesson."

"It isn't safe, Elias. If the army ..."

"I'm finished!" Moussa raises his paper, and waves it like a white flag between us.

Mama smiles, ready to praise Moussa's latest creation.

But then she doesn't.

"Moussa, who's in this picture?"

"It's Elias and me ..."

"And what are you and Elias doing?"

She flips the page around and we are met with a picture of two men, with heavy black beards, and semi-automatics slung menacingly around their shoulders.

"We're shooters, Mama. And we're going to grow up to protect you and Baba."

Baba removes the sheet from Mama's trembling hands, examines it, and then crumples it into a tight ball.

Confusion darkens Moussa's bright eyes and his face begins to fall. Where are the words of praise? Where is the tape that will fix this square onto the refrigerator's quilt?

Moussa begins to cry and Baba bends down to console him.

"I have no doubt that you will protect us, Moussa, but it will not be with guns. It will be with education and words ..." He pauses, searching for language that his five-year-old will understand. "With kindness and acts of courage." Baba gives Moussa's shoulders a slight squeeze and stands.

"Elias, take your brother with you to play."

"Peter!" Mama protests.

"They have one childhood, Lena, and I believe the 'hood' in that word stands for protection. Not darkness."

Rafi and I run to the door and Moussa tails us. We break out into the day's blinding rays, bound through the yard, and climb through the slit in the chain-link fence that leads into the field behind our house.

We form a triangle and begin to kick the ball to one another.

Rafi's passes to me are fast and hard and my passes to Moussa are close and gentle. We clap when he kicks the ball and he jumps up and down.

"Go for the goal!" Rafi shouts, and I begin to run. I look up to the sky and find myself lost in its endless blue, struck by the thought of how far I'll have to run to find the calm it seems to promise.

"Elias! Elias!" Rafi and Moussa chant my name and I am brought back to reality just in time to see the ball bouncing toward me. I manage to control it, and with all my force, kick it through the peeling yellow posts.

Rafi and Moussa erupt into cheers.

Rafi runs over to me and scoops up the ball.

"Elias, are you going to church this afternoon? My grandmother has asked me to take her. She says it'll be safer on Friday than Sunday, when there's a bigger crowd."

I nod, then look up at a military helicopter flying overhead. Like Rafi and his grandmother, we usually attend service on Sunday, but haven't for the past few months.

The churches are being bombed, ruthlessly.

"No, Rafi. We're not."

"Okay. I'll see you on the field tomorrow!" he replies and begins to jog away.

"Rafi!" I call, over the noise of the passing chopper, and he looks back. "Be safe."

"Only God knows, Elias!" he replies with a wink and vanishes around the corner.

Later that afternoon, as I am helping Mama prepare for dinner, we hear the explosion.

Baba runs down the hall and is out the door, with me trailing close behind before Mama can stop us.

I spot the black smoke climbing two blocks to the east of us and we race toward it.

As I turn into the second street, my legs freeze. I realize that the cloud is billowing from the church.

"Elias! We must hurry," Baba shouts. "It's likely another barrel bomb." He grabs my hand and we continue running. He knows that those helping are going to need as many hands as possible.

When we reach the site, I can barely breathe, and I put my hands on my knees to catch my breath.

When I look up, Baba stands as still as a statue at my side. Together we stare at the wreckage.

There is a sea of women and children, sobbing, arms outstretched toward the church before them.

But it is no longer a church.

It is a pile of rubble.

The roof has collapsed and the once solid walls have been

reduced to heaps of stone.

A number of men have already begun to rush forward, some working together to lift the heaviest rocks, others carrying survivors to the sidewalk.

I look at the men, the women, the children in their arms—all scraped and bloodied, many missing limbs. I feel my legs begin to buckle and Baba puts a hand on my shoulder to steady me.

My father and I move to join them and begin lifting the scattered stones.

Soon we are breathless and covered in white dust.

I move to the right to lift a large, jagged piece that has been thrown from the roof, and this is when I see it.

A glint of silver.

My throat tightens and my stomach lifts. I tear into the rubble, as my fingers begin to bleed.

I do not look until I have finished.

It is a necklace.

Attached to a body.

Unrecognizable in its stillness.

"No!" My legs give way and I drop to my knees. "Rafi ..." I grab hold of his hand—the hand that had so recently curled into a fist for my run ... that had just high-fived me after my goal.

It is now cold and does not squeeze me back.

"Elias!" Baba sees my despair and drops the stone he is holding. He pushes himself to his feet and stumbles over the fallen rock as he makes his way toward me.

Once at my side, he follows my gaze, transfixed and horrified. Realization floods his face and his eyes close.

Taking a long, broken breath, he opens his eyes. He motions to the men who have taken on the role of collecting the dead: the ones lying limp in their arms, the ones being placed in a separate section, the ones being wrapped in sheets of white cloth.

Then, without warning, he slings my arm over his shoulders.

"I am not a survivor!" I want to scream. But there is no energy and no words for it.

Only the sickening feeling that I will never survive the death of my best friend.

Baba manages to get me home and places me in my bed. I can hear him speaking softly and rapidly to my mother. And then I hear her sobs, muffled, as she collapses on his shoulder.

For the next few days, Mama keeps the blinds closed. Not as a reflection of my mood, or my mourning, but to make sure that I do not see the stray dogs, who for days have been eating the dead bodies.

CHAPTER 4

CANADA

Elias steps out into the early winter air and shivers. He pauses, listening for the sound of the mortar shells. Then he shakes his head, remembering that he is no longer in Syria.

He gently closes the door to his Aunt Eva's house and makes his way down the driveway that is dusted with snow.

He steps onto the sidewalk that will take him the three short blocks to school, then tugs up the zipper on his new coat and plunges his hands into his pockets. When he first arrived from Syria, he didn't own a winter coat. And although it was nice of his aunt's church to donate one, he wishes he didn't have to wear it.

Elias hates the weather here: the biting cold, the relentless wind, the endless gray.

He thinks back to Syria, to the sun that saturated the sky, and exhales deeply.

Seeing his breath before him only makes him feel worse.

Despite having been in Canada for the past three months, Elias still feels the ache in his chest. Often, he imagines his heart as a stereo, and his pain a volume knob that his memories control. The volume varies, depending on the day, the time, and the trigger. When the trigger is swift and unexpected, it feels as though the bass has been cranked, and a pain that almost blinds him reverberates throughout his entire body.

As Elias rounds the corner and steps onto the school's lawn, an icy white ball flies past his eyes.

"Duck!" someone shouts and he is pulled to the ground.

"You were almost fatally wounded!" Liling laughs. "The first snowfall of the year—and in November! There was no stopping this snowball fight!"

Elias rises and Liling tugs him back down.

"They're in the middle of a battle! There's no way you're getting through the front door."

He looks up to the cement steps leading into the school and sees Josh and Ben. They're acting as commanders on either side of the doors, directing their troops to attack any Grade 9's trying to enter.

"What are you doing down here?" he asks. From the impression he sees in the snow, it looks as though Liling has been lying there.

"I'm making a snow angel." She smiles. "See?" She rolls to the left, and sure enough, in the space where she'd been lying, is an imprint of a perfect angel, its wings wide and far-reaching.

"Oh … cool." Elias feels himself smiling.

Liling's eyes light up. "Have you never made one?"

He shakes his head, thinking the closest he ever got to a snow angel was the sight of his father covered in white sand, after the rocket-propelled grenade exploded.

"No worries! It's easy. You just lie down and swish your arms and legs around." She moves into a fresh spot and motions him over. "Here, try it."

"Nah," he says, feeling self-conscious.

"Come on," Liling urges. "We have to neutralize this war."

Reluctantly, he lies down and begins to swish his arms and legs in and out. He's no angel, but in a war, he knows you can't lie still. You have to do something.

Soon the vice principal emerges and hauls Josh and Ben into her office. Elias and Liling climb the concrete stairs into the school and make their way to English class.

Ms. McKeown stands at the classroom door, a smile on her face, greeting each student as he or she enters.

So far, Elias thinks English is all right. He likes getting lost in other people's stories.

"Good morning, class," Ms. McKeown begins, shushing the chatter in the room. "I'd like to begin by discussing next week's field trip."

Ms. McKeown is big on what she calls experiential learning.

To mark the beginning of their poetry unit, she has written on the board: *How can we know the dancer from the dance?* It's a line from her favorite poet, Yeats.

"Remember, class," Ms. McKeown tells them, "an author is never far removed from his or her writing. As writers, who you are, what you've experienced, is woven within your every word." She pauses, letting her point sink in. "So before you write your winter poem," she continues, a smile tugging at her lips, "we'll be taking a field trip to Toronto, to go skating at Nathan Phillips Square."

"Oh, great," mutters Sullivan, who had begun sitting next to Elias each day. "I hate physical activity."

Elias shakes his head and smiles. He has come to tolerate Sullivan. There's an innocence about him, an openness that makes him seem much younger than Elias. He likes Sullivan's enthusiasm and the way he exclaims, "You gotta see this!" before showing him a viral video—the latest one of a sneezing panda. Elias especially likes the drawings he does when Ms. McKeown is droning on. In the margins of his notebook, Sullivan makes little cartoons of his classmates, imagining them as the characters in whatever book or play they're reading. Yesterday, he drew Elias as Romeo. He was at the Capulet masquerade, his arm outstretched to a beautiful girl with long dark hair.

"You're hysterical." Elias rolled his eyes.

"That's not what Liling thinks," Sullivan responded.

"I doubt that ..." Elias's brows furrowed, confused at his response.

"Every girl likes a man of mystery, and she really doesn't know a thing about you," said Sullivan, shrugging his shoulders and shading in the mask he had just finished drawing on Romeo's face.

"Okay, class." Ms. McKeown calls for their attention. "To get inspired for our upcoming field trip, I'd like you to take out your journals." She moves to the side of the whiteboard to reveal their topic, neatly printed in its center: *My First Memory of Winter* ...

The class groans.

"Think snowflakes, tobogganing, hot chocolate ..." she lists, enthusiastically. "Follow the memory, wherever it might lead!" Elias looks down at the page before him and at his hand, which has begun writing the words of the coldest—cruelest—memory he has of Syria.

A memory he knows he isn't ready to revisit.

CHAPTER 5

SYRIA

Today, as on so many days since the war began, I woke to the sound of my parents arguing in the kitchen.

I rolled out of bed, crept down the stairs, and leaned against the wall that separates the hall from the kitchen.

The power was out and the room was dimly lit. I saw the beginnings of sunlight peeking through the curtain of the small window above the sink.

"Peter," my mother said, "you can't keep doing this."

"Lena, I'm fine," Baba replied.

"You need your strength, Peter. What if the army attacks your clinic or the rebels try to recruit you?"

"Then you and Elias will have the energy to protect yourselves and Moussa."

"Please, Peter." I sensed Mama trying to take something from Baba's hands, and peered around the corner before he could move it away.

It was his brown leather belt.

He leaned over the counter and a ray of sun glinted off the

scalpel he was holding in his right hand.

With precision, he twisted the blade in a circular motion, eventually removing a tiny, round piece of hide.

"Peter …" Mama placed a hand on Baba's shoulder and looked him directly in the eye. "We're almost out of supplies. I know we've been avoiding the market, for fear of mortar shells and stray bullets. But we no longer have that option. Our basket of food is nearly empty—we need a new one."

"Lena, the roads for humanitarian access are being targeted by the government. I doubt any new baskets have made it through."

Baba untucked his shirt and pulled it up, exposing his middle.

"We need to try," Mama pleaded.

I stared open-mouthed at Baba's stomach.

There was no longer the soft paunch I remember resting my head against when stories of adventure were being told. Instead, I saw a lean middle, ribs showing, that had begun to cave inward.

Baba sighed, took the belt and wound it, not around his pants, which had been secured with a knotted plastic IV tube from his clinic, but higher, beneath his ribcage.

"Then we will go this morning," he replied reluctantly, and fastened the belt in its new, tighter hole. It was there to dull the hunger pangs I could only imagine he was feeling.

"Elias," my father says sternly, as he buzzes about the room, ensuring that the curtains are closed and the doors are locked. "We'll be back shortly."

I nod, feeling my stomach fill with dread over the dangers that await them.

"Take the usual precautions," he says, and I nod my head again as they open the door and leave.

The door has barely closed behind them when I hear Moussa's little feet coming down the stairs.

"Good morning, Moussa," I say and force a smile. I know that he will be upset that Mama and Baba aren't here.

"Good morning, Elias," he replies. His wide eyes sweep the rooms for our parents.

"They went on a very special mission," I say, before he can ask his worried question.

Moussa's eyebrows rise and his mouth opens into a little "o."

"Do you know what they've gone to find?" I ask.

Moussa shakes his head happily from side to side, hoping for a surprise.

"They've gone to find Ema'a," I say. I know the thought of the Syrian ice cream, sprinkled with pistachios, will make him happy.

Moussa jumps up and down. "Are we celebrating?" he asks. We only have it on special occasions.

"Yes, Moussa! We are celebrating ... Family Day," I fib.

"Family Day?" he asks.

"Yes, celebrating our family being all together, of course. Now could there be a better reason to celebrate than that?" I ask, moving in to tickle him.

"No-o-o!" he squeals, trying but failing to escape my grasp.

"You are my prisoner!" I say, imitating Baba's deep voice as I hold him in my arms. "I will release you, but only for a hefty ransom."

"An-y-th-ing!" he manages to squeak out between giggles.

"One drawing," I say, slowing my fingers. "A Moussa original." I let him roll out of my reach, his smile fading as the memory of his last drawing being destroyed returns to him.

"Come," I say, leading him to the table, "and we will think of something to draw together."

Moussa sits at the table, a fresh sheet of paper before him. As I am laying his markers down, we hear a long trilling and our eyes travel to the front window.

"Elias, did you hear that?" Moussa asks.

I am about to say I hadn't, when the trilling sounds again, this time in a jingling refrain.

We move to the window and open the curtain slightly. It reveals a small bird, perched on a branch, no more than twenty feet from our house.

I lean into the window's sill. "It's a serin, Moussa," I reply. I recall a long-ago lesson on Syrian wildlife and remember that the once-stable species of finch is now very vulnerable.

"Mama's favorite?" he asks.

"Yes, that's right."

"Elias," Moussa says, looking to the fridge, to the one empty square in the quilt. "I will draw the serin!"

I smile at his desire to make our mother happy.

"What a great idea," I reply. Then I lead Moussa back to the table.

He is no sooner seated than a sadness washes over his face.

"Go ahead, Moussa," I say, and give his markers a light tap.

He looks down at them and then back up at me. "I don't remember its colors."

I think back to Baba's words about childhood: *The hood is for protection, Lena, not darkness.* Surely we will be fine in front of the house.

"We can go take a quick look, Moussa," I say, firmly. "But it will be there and back, understood?"

Moussa bobs his head up and down, and wraps his arms around himself, as though trying to contain his inner glee.

"Shhh, Moussa," I say as we approach the tree. "If we make a noise or move quickly, we scare him away."

When we are a little more than three feet from the serin, I place my hand on Moussa's shoulder to stop him from moving closer.

"There," I whisper and point to the branch where the serin sits. "Can you see its colors?"

Moussa nods intently as he gazes at the bird. I know he's making a mental note of its feathers—a mixture of yellow, gray, and black—and its beak, which shimmers silver in the morning light.

The serin begins to flutter its wings and, right when we think it's about to fly, it stops, and hops to another, sturdier branch instead.

Moussa begins to flap his arms gently. "Elias," he says, as he hops to his right, "wouldn't it be wonderful if we had wings?"

I look back to the bird and think of my friends and their families. I think of the many who have been forced to flee Syria on foot for Jordan, Turkey, or Lebanon.

Staring at the serin, I begin to remember why it's in danger. Humans have ruined its environment: cutting down its trees, eating its vegetation, stealing its water ...

I reach out to the bird and realize how similar we are. Our home is being demolished, our people displaced and dying. We are also endangered, I say silently to the serin. And this war could one day lead to our extinction.

"Elias!" Moussa screams.

I jerk my head to the right and catch a flash of camo and a Syrian flag on an arm clutching my little brother.

"Moussa!" I begin to shout.

But his name is barely out of my mouth when the soldier's comrade strikes me in the head with the butt of his revolver and everything turns black.

CHAPTER 6

CANADA

The school bus is a riot.

Students are shouting across the aisles, while others bounce up and down in their seats.

Elias sits near the front and looks out the window, his eyes fixed on a German Shepherd taking an early morning walk with its owner.

Ms. McKeown turns around and shushes the students before looking back at the school and then impatiently checking her watch.

The bus is waiting for Liling and Sullivan, who have run back to their lockers to grab their cameras. They want to take pictures of the field trip for the school yearbook.

Elias sees Ms. McKeown's shoulders relax and looks over to see Sullivan and Liling climbing into the bus.

Sullivan stops to survey his options.

Two seats remain. One near the front, next to Elias, and the other closer to the back over the wheel, where it's hard to fit two people comfortably.

Sullivan walks down the aisle and stops by Elias, before turning to Liling behind him.

"Liling, I'll grab the one over the wheel—you sit with Elias," he says, and winks at him before continuing on his way.

"Hey, Elias—sorry to squish you." Liling drops into the space beside him and swings her knapsack onto her knees.

"That's okay," he says, feeling his stomach begin to knot.

He stares at Liling's bag, a collage of symbols and quotes, then searches for something to say.

"What does that mean?" he asks, pointing to a stitched patch on the front pocket.

"It's the Chinese symbol for strength," she answers. "Boy, did I ever need that when I first came to Canada."

"You weren't born here?" he asks, surprised.

Liling shakes her head. "No, my family emigrated from Jiangsu, China, when I was in the sixth grade. I was in ESL in elementary school and this is actually my first year taking mainstream English."

"Oh ..." Elias says, shocked. "I would never have known that it wasn't your first language."

"Really? I still worry sometimes about my accent, but I worked really hard in school and took classes in the evenings and on weekends. It was so hard when I first arrived, not being able to communicate, not being able to connect ..." She shakes her head and sighs. "Sullivan was actually my first friend here. He would pass me these notes, but instead of writing inside, there'd be a picture, and then I'd respond with one of my own." She begins to smile. "That's what I love about art—it's a universal language." She grins. "How did your English become so good?"

"My mom worked as a translator back home."

"That's really cool," Liling replies. She's about to ask another question when they hear the shouting.

Elias and Liling turn just in time to see an empty water bottle sailing toward Sullivan's head.

"Cut it out!" he shouts, before slumping further into his seat.

Josh, Ben, and the other boys at the back erupt into laughter.

"I should have taken that seat," Liling says, then turns back and bites down on her lip. "Sullivan told me that they've bullied him since the third grade. It got so bad that his parents had to home-school him for Grades 7 and 8. He wanted to come back so badly this year. I guess with it being high school, fresh start and all …"

"Fresh start?" Elias says, abruptly cutting her off. "There's no such thing."

"You really believe that?" she asks, sadness in her voice. "People can learn from their experiences …" she says, pausing. "I think they can begin again."

Elias shakes his head. "People are their experience," he says, looking back at Sullivan, slumped in his seat. "And where they go, it goes with them."

The bus pulls up in front of Nathan Phillips Square and Elias and Liling get off. They wait off to the side and Liling waves to Sullivan as he steps onto the sidewalk.

Elias, Liling, and Sullivan turn to follow Ms. McKeown and the other students in the direction of the outdoor skating rink.

Elias spins slowly in a circle to take in the city around him. He has never been to Toronto. The skyscrapers and the hustle and bustle of the crowds remind him of the trips he made to Damascus with his father when he'd begun to run low on medical supplies.

Elias, Sullivan, and Liling stop, taking in the huge sheet of ice before them. "This totally beats being at school," Liling says, smiling. "Let's grab a seat …" She looks at Elias and notices that he isn't carrying a bag. "Elias, there's a rental shop there and you can meet Sullivan and me on that bench," she says and points to her right.

Elias nods and makes his way over to the small shop. He looks at the sign on the counter: *Adult Skate Rentals $10, Helmets $5.* Elias reaches into his pocket and handles the twenty dollar bill his mother had given him that morning, insisting that he wear a helmet.

"What size do you need?" the storekeeper asks Elias.

"Maybe a 10 …" Elias replies.

"Do you want a helmet?" he asks.

Elias looks over to the rink, where many of his classmates have already begun skating, gliding effortlessly across the ice.

"No," Elias says. His stomach flips as he realizes this will put an even bigger target on his back.

He gives the man his money and dumps the change in his pocket.

As he walks back to Liling and Sullivan, he feels a wave of homesickness wash over him. He wishes he were on a field, his feet firmly planted in moist, squishy earth.

Liling watches the skaters go round, and Sullivan stares into his phone while Elias laces up his skates. After standing to face them, he sees Sullivan glance at his feet.

"Whoa! Elias!" Sullivan points at his laces, which he has tied loosely so that he can take off the skates as quickly as possible. "Unless you have ankles made of steel, you're going to fall right over! Have a seat," Sullivan instructs and kneels down before him. "You have to tie them super tight …" he pulls strongly on the laces, "… or, trust me, you won't be able to stand up straight."

"In my case, I don't think it'll make a difference," Elias replies.

Liling laughs. "You'll be fine," she assures him.

Elias walks to the edge of the ice and stops. Sullivan steps on the ice and skates off, camera around his neck, beginning to snap shots of the students whirling by.

Liling steps confidently onto the ice and turns around to face him.

"Here, Elias," she says, holding up her red mittens. "Hold on to my hands."

He looks around and notices that most of the other guys are at the opposite end of the rink. They skate to the edge and turn to their sides to stop, seeing who can scrape off as much ice as possible.

He hesitates and then grabs her hands as they step cautiously onto the ice.

"There you go," she says with a smile. "Now, just think: push and glide, push and glide." Liling lets go to demonstrate. She then grabs his hands again, while he attempts his first few moves. "You're a natural!" she says, sounding genuinely impressed.

Soon, Elias is managing on his own. His glides are more like wobbles and he's pretty sure his only means of stopping is a slow slide to the edge and a roll on the pavement, but he doesn't look quite like the baby deer he had envisioned.

"Looking good, Elias!" Ms. McKeown calls, her ponytail blowing in the wind as she breezes past.

Liling skates back over to Elias and does a little twirl before stopping in front of him.

"You're doing great, Elias," she says, joining him so that they are skating side by side.

"So you speak English and skate perfectly?" Elias asks. "You must be on every immigration poster."

Liling laughs, but he can tell she's thinking about this. "Well, let's just say it didn't happen overnight." She looks up, taking in the white sky around her. "When we first arrived, my cousin was studying at the University of Toronto. When we'd visit, our parents would have tea, and he'd take me skating. See these?" she says, pointing to the three cement arches above their heads. "They're called the Freedom Arches. My cousin said they were dedicated to the Canadians who fought for or defended the country's freedom."

Elias looks up, as they sail easily underneath.

"Oh, I better go snap that for them," Liling says, noticing a group of girls off to the side, shaky on their skates, trying to take a group selfie.

Liling skates away and Elias wants to take a break, even if it might involve a belly flop onto the concrete. Josh, Ben, and two other boys from his English class begin to circle around him.

"Whoa, dude!" Josh hollers, as he puts his arms out to the side, mimicking Elias's unsteadiness on the ice. "You need to put training wheels on those things." The boys tighten their circle and begin to skate dizzyingly around Elias.

"Now!" Josh yells, and the boys come to a swift stop with their right legs spraying him with a burst of snow.

Shaky and disoriented, Elias can no longer keep his balance. Before he knows it, his skates are flying and his arms are flailing, and there is nothing but frigid air to grab onto.

Elias lands with a thud on the unforgiving ice below, the sound of laughter ringing in his ears.

CHAPTER 7

SYRIA

"Moussa!" I call, panic in my chest. I am awake but everything is dark.

I feel a little hand settle itself on mine and my body relaxes.

"No talking!" A voice in the darkness shouts and the panic resumes full force.

I sense someone hovering and I try to lash out. It is at this moment that I realize my hands have been tied in front of me. I quickly move my body to the left to shield my little brother.

"Stop moving!" the voice shouts, and I feel its owner reach behind my head and untie the firm knot on my blindfold.

"Kamal," a commanding voice calls, "we need you in Room Three."

The soldier leaves before he can untie Moussa's blindfold.

I wince as my eyes adjust to the harsh fluorescent lights, and I hear the door close behind me.

I whirl my head to the left, to make sure I hadn't imagined that small hand on mine.

I haven't, and there Moussa sits, beside me, his body rigid, a bandana pulled tightly over his eyes.

I give him a once-over and he seems to be all right. Aside from his wrists which, like mine, are reddened from the plastic cord that binds them together.

Hurriedly, I move my hands to his bandana, but am stopped by a terrible sound. It is the sound of whacking, followed by the shrill cries of screaming children.

Quickly, I return my hands to my lap, leaving Moussa's bandana in place. The less he ends up seeing, the better, I think. If only I could cover his ears …

I take a deep breath and try to calm my racing heart. For the first time since my blindfold was removed, I take in the room around me.

A wave of shock hits me. The place is familiar.

We are in a clinic.

And it is our father's.

Moussa and I sit in the small waiting room out front. The cries, now whimpers, are coming from behind the door to the left, which leads to the four small patient rooms beyond.

There is a dull ache coming from where I'd been struck in the head. I bring my hands to my temple and feel dried blood flake onto my fingertips.

I look around the room, at its familiar beige walls and brown floors. We sit in two of the six worn waiting chairs on this side of the wall, with another six empty ones facing us. The thought of what we are waiting for grips me.

The whacking begins again—this time more fierce—and I know we are not waiting to be healed.

They have barricaded the door with boxes of medical files from Baba's office.

Near the top of these boxes, a child's picture of a sea turtle peeks out.

"My patients always tell me how much better they feel when they come and see me," Baba said to Mama, when he arrived home one day. "I think it is Moussa's artwork that is the true healer. When I go into the waiting rooms, I see my patients looking at his pictures ... and for a moment, they're lifted from their worries by the innocence, the lightness of childhood, and the memories they must be reminded of."

I had looked over at Moussa, who was smiling sheepishly, before he scurried up to his bedroom to begin his next creation.

I wonder how many children they have trapped behind that door, imprisoned with Moussa's cheery images.

I remember a night a few months back, right before we lost connection to the Internet. I was in my room, playing a game on my laptop, long after my parents had told me to go to bed. Once I'd finished, I went online to the news site, Al Arabiya, and the headline "Syrian Government Detaining and Torturing Its Children" glowed in the darkness. At first, I refused to click on it, fearing that somehow that would make it true. But I couldn't resist and, before long, I was reading about the army arresting children whose parents were wanted—and then starving, beating, and shocking them with electricity for what they knew.

I look over now at Moussa in the chair, his legs dangling, unable to reach the floor. What could he possibly know? But it isn't what he knows, I realize. It's what he's heard, or what the soldiers think he might have heard. Children running through the streets are small enough to be hidden or overlooked during important conversations.

Vulnerable, scared, weak, and truthful, we have naturally become the best source of intel.

I am brought out of my thoughts by the sound of the door opening. A man in camouflage carries a young boy, limp in his arms. He drops him on the floor before returning the way he came, slamming the door behind him.

The boy is lying face down and does not move. I look closely at his arms, spotted with small burns the size of a cigarette end, down to his hands, where I see there are three fingernails missing.

A paralyzing shiver runs down my spine.

"Elias?" Moussa says as he turns his blindfold toward me, terror in his voice.

"Yes, Moussa?"

"Are we jasmines being planted in the garden?"

"No, Moussa," I say, and reach my wrists over to cup my hands tightly around his. "It's winter here."

CHAPTER 8

CANADA

Elias lies on the ice, unmoving.

He is looking up at the Freedom Arches, thinking they are miles from his reach, when a red mitten blocks his view.

Instinctively, he reaches up and is pulled to his feet by Liling.

"Elias, what happened?" she asks, her eyes wide.

"Nothing," he replies. "I just fell."

Liling looks at him skeptically as he brushes the snow from his jeans. She skates behind him and removes the flakes of ice from his back.

"Everyone falls their first time," she says, returning to face him. "I'm sure it was very graceful!"

Despite the anger and embarrassment Elias is feeling, a laugh escapes his lips.

"Let's skate it off," Liling says. "We'll go for a few more rounds and then we'll take a break," she promises and motions him back into the loop of skaters.

"Those guys are just the worst," she says, once they've woven themselves in, jutting her chin toward Josh and his friends. Elias looks over to the bench where they're unlacing their skates, wiping the snow from their blades and whipping it at each other.

"Haven't they gotten in trouble yet?" Elias asks, as he remembers the punishment he would have received if he had acted that way back in Syria.

"They're pretty sly," Liling says. "Always waiting for the moment when no one's watching ... when the teacher's back is turned." She shakes her head, overcome with anger. "And don't even get me started about online; it's like a black hole in our universe."

It isn't right, Elias thinks, hurting people who haven't done anything to them, using others for their own selfish ends ... his mind begins to drift back to Syria.

"Hey, guys!" Sullivan shouts, coming up from behind them and turning to skate backward once he's past. "I think this is the most physical activity I've gotten all year!" He begins to pant heavily, pretending he's going to collapse. "I don't think I can go on much longer," he gasps. "Liling, if this is it ..." he kneels on the ice and extends his arm to her. "I want you to ..."

Liling raises her eyebrow in amusement.

"... have my Xbox," he spits out.

"Oh, how very thoughtful," she replies, rolling her eyes. "Well, Elias. I think the only thing that's going to bring Sullivan back to life is a hot chocolate."

Sullivan stands, his energy having miraculously returned. "I'll go," he says, "as much as it pains me to leave the ice."

"Elias, do you want one?" he asks.

Elias reaches into his pocket for his change, but hesitates, thinking his mother might need it later. "It's okay," he's about to say, when Sullivan interrupts.

"Don't worry about it," Sullivan says, skating away. "My treat."

Elias is about to protest, but Liling begins to speak.

"You're going to love it," Liling says. "Tim's makes the best hot chocolate."

"Oh," Elias says, confused, "is that a friend of Sullivan's?"

Liling laughs, "He wishes! No, it's a coffee shop named after Tim Horton—he was a famous Canadian hockey player."

Elias nods, feeling foolish as he makes the connection to all those red and white signs he's seen across Richmond Hill.

He looks at Liling, confused by her happiness.

"What do you like so much about this country?" he asks, feeling like he doesn't understand. He wobbles on his skates ... like he doesn't belong.

"Well, I like the fresh air, the snow days ..."

"Snow days? You mean the days when it snows?"

"No, silly." Liling laughs. "The days when they cancel school because of the snow."

"That's a thing?" Elias says, feeling pleasantly surprised.

"It's one of the best things," she replies.

"Don't you miss China?"

"Sure. Well ..." Liling looks ready to go on but hesitates. "We better go meet Sullivan. He's probably on his way back," she says, and they begin to make their way toward the bench where they left their boots.

As they near the edge, Liling turns backward and skates in front of Elias, turning her toes inward to come to a complete stop. She places her hands on Elias's biceps, and he grabs her arms in return, feeling himself slow down and his heart speed up.

Liling steps over the edge and helps him off the ice.

Once they're sitting on the bench, they begin to undo their skates.

"Well, they're much easier to get off than put on," Elias says, as he removes his second one and ties the pair's laces into a loose bow.

"Did you want to return yours now?" Liling asks, as she tucks her own into her knapsack.

"Nah," Elias says, not wanting to keep Sullivan waiting, "I'll just throw them over my shoulder and return them on our way back."

"Careful of the blades," Liling says. "They should really come with skate guards."

"I should come with skate guards," Elias replies and Liling laughs.

Elias smiles, feeling a faint, forgotten emotion, and they begin their walk to the corner of Bay and Queen.

"I actually thought he would have been back by now," Liling says, checking the time on her phone as they make their way along the crowded street.

They stop at the crosswalk and Elias spots Josh and his gang on the other side, each devouring a box of Timbits.

The light goes green and they begin to cross.

As they pass Josh and Ben, Elias feels the anger returning to his chest.

"Your hot chocolate's getting cold," Josh says, smirking.

Liling gives Elias a puzzled look and is about to speak, when she sees something past his shoulder.

Her eyes widen and she begins to run.

"Liling!" Elias shouts, unsure of what's happening. He takes off through the crowded street after her.

And then he sees him.

Sullivan.

Slumped against the side of the building, his nose bleeding, a dark bruise spreading over his left eye.

Hot chocolate stains his hoodie and jeans, and a tray, containing three large cardboard cups, lies overturned at his feet.

"Sullivan!" Liling cries.

"I'm okay," he gasps.

For a moment, Elias cannot move.

He cannot speak.

He can only stare at the burn marks on Sullivan's arm—the small red circles where the scorching liquid splashed as the tray flipped from his fingers.

Liling crouches, attempting to help Sullivan to his feet. As she does, Elias begins to run.

He runs without thinking or feeling, back the way he came, down the street and across the next.

Elias runs until he can see Josh's back approaching the rink, and he quickens his speed until he is within reach.

And then, like a leopard freed from its cage, he pounces.

Elias turns Josh onto his back so that he can see his face and begins to punch him.

Over and over.

Again and again.

Ben and the other boys try to intervene, struggling to get him off their friend. But they are unable to break Elias's iron grip.

Slowly, they back away, as if from a madman, a fearful look in their eyes.

Elias's skates have fallen from his shoulder and lie untied next to Josh. Holding onto the collar of Josh's coat, he grabs one with his free hand and presses the blade to his enemy's throat.

Somewhere in the distance, Elias hears his name being wailed. He stops to listen. And in that moment, a strong pair of hands grips his shoulders and peels him away from the beaten and bloodied boy who lies unmoving beneath him.

CHAPTER 9

SYRIA

Moussa and I have been kept awake all night.

Screams have continued to crash over our ears before being washed away into terrifying silence.

When they stop at last, our heads become heavy and begin to nod. And when they do, the door opens and the soldier returns. "No sleeping!" he shouts, violently shaking our shoulders.

This is another form of torture, I realize. The longer we're kept awake, the lower our resistance.

I look over at Moussa, who sits whimpering, tears streaming beneath his bandana.

"Elias," he whispers.

"Yes, Moussa?"

"I'm tired ... and hungry."

"I know. I am, too ... but just think, when we get home, there will be Ema'a for us. And I bet Mama will let you have seconds."

A weak smile appears on his dry lips.

I can only imagine what Mama and Baba must be thinking. What they must be feeling. To return with relief in their hearts and supplies in their hands, only to discover an empty house—their children vanished.

I think of the fear they must have felt when they called out and no one answered. The dread, as they discovered each room empty. The hopelessness, when they found the hole in the garden unfilled.

And finally, I think of the anger, the fury they must feel at me for being so stupid. For not doing what I was told. For not protecting my little brother.

I'm torn from my thoughts by the sound of a voice, loud and powerful, questioning, and another, low and broken, responding. The lights, already dim in the clinic, flicker, and I hear a hair-raising scream.

"Elias!" Moussa shouts. "What was that?"

"Not to worry, Moussa," I reply. I'm trying to sound calm, but I fear the soldiers are using electric shock on the children behind the door.

"Just someone afraid of the dark. Someone not as brave as you. You're not afraid of the dark, are you?"

Moussa bites his lip and then slowly shakes his head.

"I didn't think so," I say. "You can see in the dark, can't you?"

From Moussa's drawings, I know that he's always seeing pictures in his mind's eye.

"What can you see?" I whisper.

Moussa pauses. "Do you remember when Baba took us into Damascus the day before Mama's birthday, to buy her a present?"

"Yes, Moussa," I reply, thinking back to that sunny day in May.

"And remember the man on the street?"

"Yes," I say again, recalling the homeless man on the corner, selling embroidered wall hangings, faded and dusty from endless hours under the sun.

"Remember, Elias, how he was lying on the ground and everyone kept passing him by?"

"Mmm hmm," I reply.

"And when we came closer, Baba put out his arms to stop us and he bent down to see if the man was okay."

"Yes, Moussa."

"And he was so red ... but he was still wearing a coat. Baba felt his forehead and said the man was burning up."

"That's right."

"Baba gave the man his hand and moved him into the shade of the bookstore. He helped him sit up, took out his handkerchief and poured the rest of his water over it, and wiped the man's forehead. Then Baba asked for my water bottle and gave it to the man to drink. And that was okay because I knew he was really thirsty."

"That was nice of you, Moussa," I say.

"Then Baba sent you into the shop to use the phone to call the ambulance."

I nod. "And we thought it was never going to come." I continue Moussa's story, remembering the congestion of the hot city streets and the rapid breathing of the man sitting at our feet. "And to take his mind off feeling sick, Baba told him all about

Mama's garden. Her lavender hyacinths, her white orchids, and her prized pink damask roses that he said she talked to when nobody was looking. Thankfully, this made the man laugh and his breathing started to slow."

"Yeah," Moussa says. "And Baba told the man why we were there, to get Mama a necklace with a small emerald, so that no matter where she went, she would always have her garden with her."

"And remember, Elias, when the ambulance finally came?"

"Yes," I reply.

"And they lifted the man onto the stretcher and he began to cry. I thought it was because he was so happy that help had arrived, but he grabbed Baba's hand and told him that he was sorry, that all of the shops were now closed. I thought Baba would be so sad, but he smiled and told the man not to worry, that he would just add his name to one of my drawings, and Mama would shake her head and forgive him. As the man was being wheeled to the ambulance, he shouted, 'Wait!'"

I nod, and then remember the man reaching into his worn jacket and removing one of his small wall hangings, stitched with the most vibrant purples, whites, and pinks.

"It was my daughter's favorite," he said.

Baba reached for his wallet but the man raised his hand. "For your wife," he insisted.

"When Mama opened her gift and Baba told her how he got it," Moussa says excitedly, "she wiped a tear from her eye, saying it was the best gift anyone could ever ask for. I think she liked it even more than the emerald!"

"Thank you for the memory, Moussa," I say, as I recall Mama hanging the work of art in our home.

"A reminder," she'd said. She took a step back, admired her gift for a moment, then fastened it to our front door with great care.

Moussa has not spoken in some time, and I am certain that he's fallen asleep. I'm grateful that he's finally in a place of dreams and not nightmares.

His memory guided me out of my dark thoughts, but its light was only a flicker. I feel myself sinking back into thoughts of what lies behind that door.

I must think, I say to myself.

When did the soldiers zero in on the clinic? Why had they decided to target it? And most importantly, did they know it was Baba's?

A feeling of dread fills my stomach and threatens to empty it as the realization hits.

First, electricity and water, then schools, churches, and hospitals; that's how you empty a village, how you rip out its organs.

The door bursts open and I am wrenched from my thoughts.

A soldier enters, his face beaded with sweat, a vein throbbing in his forehead.

"You think you're going to sleep?" the soldier says, shaking Moussa roughly. "You're going to sleep peacefully while your father helps the opposition? How many extremists has your father healed?" He shakes Moussa again, this time hitting his head against the wall. "Huh? How many rebels has he let live another day to destroy us?"

Moussa sits silently, frozen with fear.

"What, you can't count? Well, let's take you to the back, where you'll learn very quickly."

He removes his battlefield knife from his pocket and begins to sever Moussa's bindings.

"One plier, two batons, three shocks," he says, a cruel smile curling his lips.

I am outside of myself, watching as the man picks Moussa up like a rag doll and throws him over his shoulder.

I wail and, with all my strength, push on my restraints. I need to break free, to run, to tackle the soldier with the ferocity of an Arabian leopard after its prey. But my legs remain tied to the chair and I am left staring at his back as he carries my little brother away.

The soldier pauses at the door, catching my eye.

"One plier, two batons, three shocks," he says again, laughing as he closes it behind him.

CHAPTER 10

CANADA

Elias sits, frozen as the ice pack on his right hand, in a worn leather chair in the principal's office.

His mother is seated next to him, her hands clasped tightly in her lap.

As the principal reviews his notes, Elias's mother glares at her son and Elias turns his attention to the degrees on the wall, each framed in dark wood. He takes in the names of the Canadian universities, wonders if they offer civil engineering. As a civil engineer, he could design and oversee the construction of buildings, roadways, and bridges. All the things his country's crumbled infrastructure would need.

"Ms. Barakat," Mr. Adriano begins. "Thank you for coming in. As you've already heard, Elias was involved in an altercation today on a field trip to Nathan Phillips Square. I was told that he attacked one of his classmates—Joshua Higgins—and was pulled off, or rather pried off, by a passerby. An ambulance was called and Joshua was taken to the hospital. The latest update from his parents is that he's suffered a broken nose, in addition to other scrapes and bruises, but is going to be okay."

Mama nods, relief softening the tight line of her mouth. "I want to apologize for my son's actions," she says. "I am not here to offer any excuses."

The weight of his mother's disappointment forces Elias to sink deeper into his chair.

"I appreciate that, Ms. Barakat. I have reviewed Elias's file and I first want to express my sympathy ... for the hardship your family has endured."

"Thank you," Mama replies.

"Now, normally, a situation such as this would warrant a severe consequence. But I learned from Elias's friends, Liling and Sullivan, that Joshua has been bullying Elias for several months."

Elias's mother shoots him a look—this is news to her.

"And prior to the incident," Mr. Adriano continues, "Joshua assaulted Sullivan. We have a zero-tolerance policy for both bullying and physical violence at our school, Ms. Barakat, so I've decided that the best course of action is to suspend both Joshua and Elias for five days. At that point, Joshua will be back, and I'll set up a meeting with all involved to get to the bottom of this. With any luck, we'll arrive at a positive resolution.

"In addition ..." The principal pauses, casting a gentle look in Elias's direction. "We'd like to connect your son to a guidance counselor who works specifically with newcomer students, who could help him identify ... and perhaps work through ... what, aside from Joshua's actions, provoked this violent reaction."

"Thank you for your understanding," Mama says, standing to shake the principal's hand. "I can assure you that nothing like this will *ever*"—she gives Elias a stern look—"happen again."

Elias follows his mother to the bus stop, one step behind her, his head down.

They enter the glass shelter and sit on the cold metal bench in silence, because what is there to say? Why would she ask why he did what he did, when she already knows the answer, when she awakens each day with the same anguish in her heart? Why say the words out loud, when the only thing they will do is shatter the glass around them?

Elias lies on his bed in the dark.

His computer casts a glow on the plate of food that sits untouched on his desk.

Aside from using the washroom, Elias hasn't left his room since they'd returned home from school yesterday afternoon.

To keep his mind off "the altercation," Elias has buried himself in his books. He completed the math homework that Mr. Connolly posted on their Google Classroom, and was so desperate for an escape that he even finished reading *Romeo and Juliet* for English. He imagined the discussion of the play's ending that would have gone on in Ms. McKeown's class, knowing his opinion would have been so different from his classmates. He understands the desire—no, more than that, the need—that Romeo and Juliet had to be together in the afterlife.

Elias decides to start working on his winter poem when he hears a knock at the door. He's about to say that he doesn't feel like talking, when it opens a crack and Liling peeks in.

"Hey, Elias," she says, sweeping a strand of hair behind her ear. "Your mom said I could come up." She leans uncertainly against the doorframe.

"Hey, Liling," he says, hopping up and doing a panicked scan of the room, making sure there's no dirty laundry in sight. "It's nice to see you. Here," he motions to his desk chair. "Come in. You can sit here."

Elias moves to his bed and takes a seat on the edge, watching Liling as she sits and begins to take in the room around her—its white walls, single bed, and nightstand—empty except for a lamp and a soccer ball, a gift from his aunt, still in its original package.

When Elias first arrived in Canada, his aunt had offered to take him to Walmart to buy a few things that would "make the room your own." At the time, he hadn't wanted the room, let alone the things, and so he'd politely declined. But now he wishes he'd taken her up on her offer. He's seen North American TV shows and he knows that kids here have rooms that are plastered with posters of favorite actors and musicians, dressers that display frames full of smiling faces, and bookshelves that boast of academic and athletic achievements.

When they left Syria, Elias hadn't had time to pack. Hadn't even thought about it. In that moment, none of that stuff had mattered. It had been just that—stuff.

"It's not much," Elias says with a shrug.

"No, it's nice. Like a blank canvas," Liling replies.

Elias can't help but think of the contrast to his life in Syria before the war. Like the Sara Shamma paintings his mom once showed him, his life had been bursting with such color. There was barely enough room for a single new stroke of the paintbrush.

"I just wanted to see how you were doing." Liling fidgets with her hands, twirling a delicate silver ring on her index finger. "Sullivan was going to come, too, but he had to stay late to work on the yearbook."

"Is he feeling better?" Elias asks.

"Oh, yeah," Liling laughs. "He thinks he looks real tough. It's been an endless stream of selfies, with filters that he says make him look," she air quotes, "'both vulnerable and strong.'"

"Oh, boy." Elias rolls his eyes.

"How are you feeling, really?" she asks, her voice softening.

"Okay ..." he pauses. "I mean, I guess I'll be ..." his eyes drift up from Liling's face to the lone picture, done in crayon, that's been pinned to the corkboard above his desk.

"It sucks being in trouble," Liling says. "Did your mom totally freak out?"

Elias shrugs. "We've been through worse," he says, his eyes falling now to the faded scars on his arm.

"Did I tell you we were in trouble when we first arrived?"

"You? Impossible." Elias laughs, thinking that never before had he met a more perfect girl.

"Mmm hmm," she replies, her face suddenly becoming serious. "I've never told anyone except Sullivan this ... but my family and I are actually refugees. We had to claim political asylum."

Elias raises his eyebrows, shocked by this revelation.

"I thought it was for your dad's work," he says.

"Well, yeah, in a way, it definitely was." Liling takes a deep breath, as if she's going to jump into the deep end of a pool, and begins.

"Back in China, my dad worked for the government ... for their intelligence agency," she says. "He was a trained scientist in Jiangsu and, seven years ago, he was asked to join their defense department as a researcher."

"Nice."

"Yeah, it came with its perks, for sure." She laughs. Then her face becomes serious once more. "But there were a lot of risks, too."

"Really?" Elias says, thinking it sounded very secure to him.

"Yeah. Especially when my dad became critical of the project he was heading."

"Oh, wow," Elias says, knowing full well the dangers of going against a government. "What was he working on?"

Liling hesitates and then slowly answers. "He was working on ballistic missiles, initially for defense purposes, and then the focus changed ... and, well, he didn't want to be involved in targeting other countries. With the information he had, he wouldn't have been allowed to quit, and if he did, it wouldn't have been safe for us in China. So, instead, my parents waited until my father had accumulated enough vacation time, and then they planned a trip for the family to visit my aunt and uncle and our cousins in Toronto. The second we stepped off the plane and into the airport, we filed our claim."

"What happened after that?" Elias asks, mesmerized by a story he had been unaware of until now.

"Well, it took us about four years to get citizenship and, during that time, we lived with my aunt and uncle. My parents enrolled in English classes at the local library and, thankfully, with the help of my uncle, my dad was able to get an IT job with a tech firm. And while he was working, my mom studied at George Brown College to become a settlement worker so she could help other newcomer families."

"That's incredible ..." Elias says, still processing this newfound information. "Your family's really brave."

Liling shrugs. "We did what we had to do." She looks at the floor and then back up at him. "And I'm sure you did, too."

Elias stares at Liling and feels their connection intensify. She was something he hadn't experienced in a long time. She was safety and softness and strength. And for the first time ever, he felt himself wanting to dive into that deep end with her.

Elias inhales.

"I had a little brother," he says and shudders.

CHAPTER 11

SYRIA

It feels as though Moussa has been gone forever, when in reality, it has been only a few minutes.

I can't breathe, I think, pulling my wrists against the restraints and gasping for air.

"Give him back!" I scream, no longer afraid of the man in camo. "I'll tell you! I'll tell you what you want to know!"

The room remains silent and I begin to cry. The thought of Moussa behind those doors makes my body limp and I drop onto my knees.

What have I done? My body begins to heave.

What terrible things are they going to do?

This is a nightmare; it must be.

I sit up and bang my back into the chair, again and again, each time with more force. But it's no use. This is a nightmare from which I'll never awaken. Like my shadow, it'll follow me forever.

If only I were with him, I think. I could soften the situation—pretend some of the reality away.

A sound erupts from behind the door and a wave of nausea hits.

"I'm here, Moussa!" I yell, before I tilt forward and vomit onto the floor. "I'm not going anywhere." My voice sputters between coughs.

I wipe my mouth on my shoulder and am overcome by a memory of the day the war began.

We were in Mr. Khaddour's Geography class and Rafi, being Rafi, couldn't sit still. His right leg was bouncing, his left fingers were tapping, and both eyes were glued to the window, on the rays of sun disappearing from the field below.

Rafi slumped in his seat and I raised an eyebrow.

He then lifted his hand, weakly.

"Mr. Khaddour," he said, sneezing. "May I go to the office to call my mother? I'm not feeling well."

Our teacher looked up over his red-framed glasses, deliberating, and then nodded.

Rafi leapt from his chair and then, realizing his mistake, stooped his shoulders and slowed his pace, winking as he passed my seat.

"Tornados," Mr. Khaddour began as Rafi left, "develop when two masses of air, one warm and one cool, meet, creating instability in the atmosphere."

He paused, collecting his thoughts. "Several conditions are required for formation. A storm ..." he stopped for a moment, looking at the darkening sky outside the window "... must be brewing. And then a trigger is necessary to drive the moist, converging winds up."

"Mr. Khaddour," Rafi said, when he returned several minutes later. "My mother has given me permission to leave school."

"That's fine, Rafi. Quietly collect your things," Mr. Khaddour replied.

He opened his mouth to continue his lecture, when Rafi interrupted. "Sir, there's one more thing. My mother would like Elias to walk me home ... to make sure I get there okay."

Mr. Khaddour paused and adjusted his silk tie as he mulled over Rafi's request. Rafi's father worked for the Ministry of Education, and it wasn't a secret that Khaddour had ambitions.

"Oh ... Mr. Icarus," Rafi's father would say with a chuckle, when we spoke of our Geography class.

"We're nearly at the end of the day," he said, looking to the clock above Rafi's head, "so I'll allow it ..." he glanced at the class to gauge their reaction, "... this once."

As I was packing my things, Mr. Khaddour continued. "Tornados, class, are accomplished killers. You will not live to post your 'F5 selfie'." He paused, amused by his own joke. "They are capable of tremendous destruction; buildings, cars, trees, and people—nothing is safe in their wake."

I grabbed my things and Rafi and I headed out the main doors to where our bicycles were locked.

"Rafi!" I said and gave him a high five before I dropped to my knees to unlock my wheels. "You sprung us!"

"It's all about playing to what people want, Elias," he said, smiling, and fastened his helmet with an easy click.

We hopped on our bikes and headed for the winding dirt path that would take us to the park.

The sky had grown darker and, within minutes it opened, showering rain onto our shoulders.

The water soaked our shirts, but it was warm and the air smelled sweet. We laughed in the joy of our freedom.

"Let's head to my house," Rafi said. "We can grab the football."

"Awesome," I exclaimed. I loved playing football in the rain. Loved the squish of the earth beneath my feet and the glide of the grass as I dove to save the ball.

As we pulled into Rafi's drive, the front door opened and his father emerged.

"Shoot," Rafi said, under his breath. "Baba, I ..." he was about to explain himself when his father interrupted.

"Not now. Both of you boys, inside." He craned his neck, looking up and then down the street. "There's been an incident."

"What happened?" Rafi asked. His father looked worried.

"The government. They've fired on the pro-democracy protesters."

"Baba, what does that mean?" Rafi asked.

"It could mean a spark, son, big enough to ignite a civil war," his father answered, before motioning us inside and bolting the door behind him.

I am jolted out of memory by the sound of the door opening. Kamal, the soldier who removed my blindfold, returns and gives me a sinister smile.

For the first time I hold his gaze. There is nothing left for me to lose.

I take in Kamal from head to toe, thinking he's quite young—maybe only five or six years older than me.

He wears his dark hair short and slicked. His uniform is pressed and his boots are polished. I look back to his chest, empty of medals.

Kamal is undecorated but, judging from his behavior, he seems hungry for recognition, for something that'll prove his worth.

I look away from the soldier to the boxes of files barricading the front door. I must try, I think to myself. For Moussa's sake, I must.

"I can give you something," I say to Kamal as I remember Rafi's idea of playing to what people want. "Something that will make your commander proud."

I see a flicker in his eyes.

"And what would that be?"

"You must first agree to a trade," I say with forced confidence. "My knowledge in exchange for the freedom of my little brother."

"And just how do I know you're telling the truth?" Kamal asks, moving closer.

"Because it's more than just words," I reply, keeping my voice strong. "It's something you can hold. Something you can give to your commander."

Kamal does not reply and I can sense him weighing the options. My guess is he doesn't have the authority to make this decision. If the information isn't true, he'll likely risk being discharged … or worse. But if the info is true, he'll be praised and maybe even promoted.

"What is it?" Kamal finally asks.

"A file," I reply.

"And what's in it?"

"Records," I say with authority, "of rebels my father treated. He filed them under a fake name, in case his clinic was seized."

Kamal looks at the boxes stacked against the front door. There could be hundreds, if not thousands, of files to go through. And even if he and his comrades were to comb through each one, would they be able to figure out which held the intel?

"And you know the name?" he asks.

"My father told his friend, so that if anything happened to my father, he could destroy it and protect our family."

"Then tell me," Kamal demands.

"It was late one night while they were having wine, and I was falling asleep … it's hazy now, but I know if I were to see it, I'd recognize it."

I continue to look the soldier in the eye, aware of what he's thinking: the search would still take time, but the chances of it being quicker and, more importantly, successful, were greater.

Kamal walks over to my chair and removes his knife. He then bends down and cuts off my ankle restraints.

"Get up," he says, pulling me to my feet.

My legs give way from having been bound for hours, and

Kamal yanks on my arm and pulls me forward.

He walks me over to where at least fifteen to twenty boxes have been piled in front of and around the front entrance.

I bend down and lift the lid off the one closest to my feet. He hasn't untied my hands and I struggle to flip through the individual files.

"We don't have time for this," he says through clenched teeth. He pulls me up and cuts the restraints off my wrists before pushing me back to the ground.

I can now separate them, to see if the folder is there.

But it isn't.

Because it doesn't exist.

Baba isn't assisting the rebels. He gives medical aid to everyone—rebels, soldiers, and civilians alike. Baba never turns away someone in need.

I start on the next box and sneak a peek at Kamal, as he looks toward the back door with impatience.

Kamal's gun is in his holster on his right hip. If I move quickly …

"Hurry up," he says quietly and I look away.

I quickly open another box and begin to flip through. This time Kamal does not turn away and I know if I make a move now, I'll be killed.

Who will fight for Moussa then? I force the thought from my mind. I must be brave.

"That's enough!" Kamal hisses, coming toward me. "You're

leading me on a foolish chase!" He grabs for my arm to take me back to my seat, but I wriggle out of his reach.

"Let me try that one," I say desperately and point to the lone blue box in the stack, behind the ones I've already opened.

Since it's a different color, Kamal agrees.

"This is your last chance," he says.

I nod, having known when I first stood on wobbly legs that it was a last chance for me and Moussa both.

I move behind the stack of boxes and hear the door to the patient rooms open.

"Where's the boy?" a soldier demands.

"I'm letting him stretch," Kamal says.

"You know the protocol," his comrade replies.

This is it, I think. I've lost my chance; one soldier was unlikely, two is impossible. I can feel the last shred of hope leave my body, like an escaped balloon from a child's hand. I turn my back to the boxes, sink to the floor, and cover my head with my arms.

For a brief second, before I am deafened by the blast, I feel the shock wave of an explosion.

Then I am flying through the air, boxes buffering me and bouncing off me, as I am thrown against the far wall.

The world goes black and I lie there, unable to move.

"Elias!" I hear my name being called.

"Elias!" It comes again, frantically.

In the confusion, I think I am being called into Heaven and hope returns that, one day, I will see Moussa again.

My legs are pinned but I can move my arms. I stretch my hand, like a corpse through a grave, up and out of the debris.

I'm here, I shout silently. Can you see me? Do you have my little brother? Is he already safe, at peace, inside?

I can feel the rubble being lifted from my legs. Then, from my torso and arms. Finally, from my face.

"Elias!" There it is again. Blinking, I see a man covered in white, and think it must be an angel.

"Elias, are you all right?"

My hearing slowly begins to return and I realize that it is not the voice of an angel. It is my father.

"My son," he says as he scoops me into his arms. "Are you hurt? Can you stand?"

I nod and he cradles me hard for several moments, before gently setting me down and steadying me, as I regain my balance.

I raise my head slightly and the first thing I see is Kamal and the other soldier. They are lying on the ground a few feet away. Next to them is the boy with the burn marks, who'd been thrown to the ground earlier. The soldiers' and the young boy's limbs are splayed at odd angles, and shards of glass and pieces of wood are sticking out of their still bodies.

I look back toward my father, sensing his question.

"Where's Moussa?" he asks, his eyes darting wildly around the room.

I turn and point a scraped arm toward the door to the patient rooms.

But the door is no longer there.

And beyond, as if they were in a house of cards, the rooms have collapsed in on themselves.

I feel myself fainting and Baba catches me. He drops to his knees, me in his arms, and begins to weep, his tears drawing tracks through the powder on his cheeks.

CHAPTER 12

CANADA

When Elias finished his story, Liling came over to the bed, sat down beside him, and hugged him. She stayed like that for several minutes, before pulling back slightly, and whispering, "I'm so sorry," into his ear.

It was the feel of that hug that got Elias back to school. It gave him the courage to attend the meeting with Joshua and Sullivan, and the strength to ignore the swirling rumors that he was a maniac.

When he first returned, he felt like Moses parting the crowds in the hall. He heard the whispers behind his back. Liling and Sullivan showed him the images being shared online.

"This one's my favorite," Sullivan said, leaning over to show Elias a picture of his face, superimposed on the body of a gladiator. A skate was on the chest of the fallen fighter at his feet and the caption, "This is Sparta!" was written underneath.

Elias kept his head down that winter, and was leaving math one day near spring when Mr. Connolly asked him to stay behind after class.

"Elias," Connolly said, waiting until Elias looked him in the eye. "As you may know, I coach the school's soccer team, and Daniel Miller is out this season with a torn ACL."

Elias nodded, uncertain why he was telling him this.

"I was thinking you could join us," Connolly said, as he perched on the edge of the desk. "Word on the street is that you have a great tackle." He smiled.

Elias was about to refuse when his teacher continued.

"Why don't you give it a try—see how it feels?"

He found himself nodding reluctantly, thinking: how could he say no to Connolly when the teacher had been nothing but kind to him?

Mr. Connolly beamed and patted his shoulder. As Elias left the room, he thought he knew what his teacher intended. Soccer would be a good outlet for his anger.

"Here's the eliminator now!" Sullivan exclaims, high-fiving Elias as he enters the room.

"Wow, nice jersey!" Liling smiles. She sets down her paintbrush and walks in front of the table, hiding the large banner she's been working on.

"Uh-oh," she says. "This doesn't mean that you're going to be ditching us for your teammates, does it?"

Elias laughs. "Let's see how this first game goes."

"I'm going to head out to save our seats," Sullivan says to Liling, grabbing his camera and slinging it around his neck.

"We'll be rooting for you." He grins, then casually punches Elias in the shoulder before heading out the door.

"Are you nervous?" Liling asks, once she hears the door click behind him.

"Yeah," Elias replies. "It's been a while since I played …"

She nods. "Well, at least the game is one thing that hasn't changed."

"Thank goodness for that," he says and Liling laughs. "What are you working on?" he asks. He tries to peek over her shoulder but she manages to block him again.

"Oh, nothing special … it's just something for an upcoming assembly."

"Nice. Can I see?" Elias asks. This winter, he'd lived to hear her say: "Ta da!" whenever she finished her latest work of art and unveiled it to him. His favorites were her monochromatic dog and her stained-glass self-portrait. Whenever he looked at them, he wondered where Moussa's talent might have taken him.

Seeing the familiar look in Elias's eyes, Liling steps aside. At the top of the banner in large letters is his name, boldly painted in the school's blue and gold colors, and beneath it, the word *Unstoppable.*

Cheers and a giggle from long ago echo in his ears and he is overcome with emotion.

"You're going to be great," Liling says, her hand on his arm.

"You always think such nice things of me," he says, shaking his head, feeling that he doesn't deserve them.

"Because they're true," she replies.

He casts his eyes down, waiting for what feels like forever, before he asks his next question. "You're not afraid of me?"

"Of you?" She raises an eyebrow. "There's a very good chance that you're the best person I know."

Elias shakes his head. "I could have done more," he says, his hands beginning to clench.

"You did everything you could," she replies, taking his hands in hers.

They stand in silence for several moments, his eyes on the banner, her eyes on him.

"Will you be in the stands?" he asks, at last meeting her gaze.

"As soon as this paint dries," she replies with a smile and, taking a deep breath, she leans forward and kisses him softly on the cheek.

"Nice assist," Josh says to Elias the next morning, as he passes him in the hall.

"Thanks," he replies, then leans self-consciously against Liling's locker.

Sullivan and Liling stare at him.

"Well, that's different," Liling finally says.

Elias shrugs, still amazed that he'd been able to assist in the goal that had won last night's match.

"Elias, are you heading to homeroom?" Sullivan asks, as he closes his locker at the sound of the warning bell.

"Sorry, Sul, I have an appointment with Ms. Boselli."

For the past few months, Elias has been meeting with his guidance counselor in her small office across from the gymnasium. At first, he'd been reluctant to talk. So instead of leaving him to sit in silence, staring at the faded posters on the wall, she'd spent the time telling him about herself.

He'd learned that her mother had immigrated to Canada when she was just nine years old, from Pinzolo, a small town in northern Italy.

During the Second World War, Ms. Boselli's grandfather had fought for Italy's resistance. Having grown up in the mountains, he was an experienced climber and used his skills to help British and American soldiers who had become separated from their units. They were in danger of becoming prisoners of war, so he guided them over the Alps and into the safety of Switzerland.

When the war ended, nothing remained. The Nazis had pillaged her grandparents' village. They took the town's metal to smelt for their guns, cannons, and tanks, and its grains and animals for food for their soldiers.

Willing to do anything to help his family, her grandfather made the decision to immigrate to Canada. A childhood friend had been able to secure him a factory job in Toronto, making ceramic tiles. One year later, her grandmother, along with her mother and her mother's younger sister, boarded an ocean liner to join him.

"My mother always said she'd never forget those two weeks

below deck," Ms. Boselli told him. "She had to care for my grandmother, who was severely seasick, and look after her little sister, who was petrified of the journey. 'We're like Noah's animals on the ark,' my mother would tell her sister, trying to comfort her, 'leaving the dangers of the old for the safety of the new; a home where the water has receded.'"

Her grandfather met them at Union Station, and he took them by bus to the tiny flat he'd rented on the top floor of an old house. And the next week, her mother started school.

"She felt like a ghost," Ms. Boselli said to Elias. "She couldn't communicate with anyone."

And so their meetings went, until he'd slowly started to tell her things about himself.

"Elias, how did your father know where to find you?" Ms. Boselli asks, after he finishes telling her the story of being held in their father's clinic.

"At first, my parents didn't know where to look," Elias replies. "They searched through the house and then the neighborhood, knocking on doors to see if anyone had seen or heard anything. But they hadn't."

She nods, waiting for him to continue.

"It was dangerous," he says, after taking a deep breath, "but they knew they had to check in town. As they were on their way there, an older man, with blood trickling down the side of his face, came running up to them.

"He shouted: 'Turn around! Get away!' He was waving his arms. 'The clinic,' he called back as he ran. 'It's been overrun!'"

"But your parents, they kept going," Ms. Boselli says.

Elias feels his eyes fill with tears, and he blinks them away. "Baba told Mama to go back home, that he would keep going.

"'They'll kill you!' Mama had screamed.

"'Lena, we're their only chance,' Baba told her. 'Get home as quickly as you can, pack us a bag, and we'll meet you there.'"

Ms. Boselli sighs. "I can't even imagine. How did your father make it to the clinic alive?"

"He'd always walked to work, and so he knew a route—his secret shortcut, he called it—that cuts in and out of the alleyways. He'd never thought of it before, but it gave him ways of hiding along the way."

Ms. Boselli nods.

"He came out pretty close to his clinic when he saw three men crouched ahead of him. One of them was in a bandana of rebel colors and he was aiming a rocket-propelled grenade at the clinic.

"My father screamed, 'Stop!' But it was too late. The RPG smashed into the clinic's wall. When the smoke cleared, he raced to the ruin, and that's when he found me, buried inside."

"You must have been in such shock," she says.

"We both were. He pulled me out and then I pulled him up. He was on his knees. His arm was still stretched out to where the patient rooms had been. We stumbled toward them, then we began to dig—we dug until our skin was torn and our nails bled—but it was no good. The RPG had destroyed everything. I heard the voices of men approaching. We couldn't stay, but how could we go?

"'Baba!' I said, but he didn't seem to hear me. He just went on digging in the debris.

"'Baba!' I tried again. 'Where's Mama?' I was sure she would have come with him. The sound of my voice pulled him out of his shock.

"'Elias,' he said, looking at me. 'Lena,' he looked toward the door. 'We have to go,' he said. He leaned down … I heard his sob … he closed his eyes … and then he kissed the rubble … my brother's grave.

"I leaned down and helped him to his feet. We stumbled through the debris … and then we ran all the way home.

"There was no time to think," Elias goes on. "The fighting had reached our neighborhood and there were warplanes dropping bombs overhead. I ripped a picture from the fridge that Moussa had drawn of the two of us—and we fled.

"Baba, Mama, and I … we walked like the undead for the remainder of the day and throughout the night—over twenty kilometers—until we reached the Lebanese border."

There was a pause.

"What happened there?" Ms. Boselli asks.

"The border guard was kind. He listened to our story, and then he drove us a few kilometers down the road to a refugee camp."

"Would you like to go on?" she asks gently.

Elias sits in silence, searching for the words to describe the torment he'd experienced. But the words don't come.

CHAPTER 13

LEBANON

I have lost track of the days.

In the camp, there is nothing to distinguish one day from the next. There is no school, no activities, no structure to our time. Our days blend together and run on, as endlessly as the rows of patchwork tents erected in the mud.

I remember the day we first arrived.

I didn't know what to expect. Of course I didn't expect there to be joy or laughter, but I thought there might be a shared sense of relief. Relief from having fled the war, from having found safety, from being alive.

But there was none.

"Welcome to the open-air prison," a shoeless man said to my father. He showed us a tent made of strung-up plastic sheets, with straw mats and pieces of pale blue fabric covering its gaps.

It didn't take long for me to understand what he'd meant.

The people here might have fled the war, but they weren't free. They were imprisoned in this camp while they anxiously awaited verdicts on asylum claims, news of private sponsorships, or the end of the war. As with most prisons, there was solitary confinement. In this one, it existed in the mind—each inmate trapped in memories of loved ones: either dead, or left behind, or gone ahead on the harrowing journey across the Mediterranean Sea.

My parents and I haven't been able to eat much since we reached the border. Food is the furthest things from our minds since losing Moussa. But it doesn't really matter, because the food here is scarce, and what can be found is rotting and it makes people sick.

Mama refuses to leave our tent, choosing instead to stare dismally out past the flap Baba opens each morning. I'm grateful she packed Baba's medical bag. Since we set up, he has been visiting tents and helping anyone he can. I think he's trying to keep his mind off Moussa, the one person he couldn't help.

I join him on these rounds because there is nothing else for me to do, and it is better than sitting in the loud silence with Mama. Baba has little with him to help people heal, but he is able to check in on those who are sick and provide them with some peace of mind, and suggest practical things they can do to get better. But some people won't get better.

We return to the tent each day before sunset. It is not safe to be out after that. There are men flashing knives, fighting, and stealing. I think we'd be okay, because of the need for Baba's medical care and his compassion—but Baba says those things did not serve us well in the past, so we close the pale blue flap, Mama's only window into the world, and try to sleep.

"You're winning," I say to my new friend, Ahmed, as we throw stones into a dusty white bucket.

He nods but does not reply.

He hasn't spoken in over a year. His older sister, Sana, tells me that the only time he speaks is in his sleep. He screams, "No! Zain!" over and over, jamming his palms against his ears, until she wakes him and pries his hands from his head.

Ahmed and I spend most of our afternoons together. We wander the camp, trying to think of things to fill the hours. Sometimes we jump the wires that anchor the tents to the ground, or we throw stones into this bucket, with its broken handle, that we found abandoned by the wire fence last week. Recently, Ahmed has begun to join my father and me on our rounds, staying close to my side for several hours. Then, I will turn to tell him something and he will be gone— sadness has called him back to his tent to lie down.

Yesterday I went to visit him, but Sana said that it was a very bad day, the anniversary of their cousin's death, and he didn't want to come out.

She sat with me instead. And as we threw stones into the bucket, she told me of their life back in Syria. Her father had been a tailor, with a small shop in Damascus, and her mother had stayed home to take care of her children "... and her vegetables," she laughed. A light comes into her eyes. "She turned our balcony into a bed of soil, growing tomatoes, peppers, green onions, you name it! Sometimes," she said, "my father gets work on this farm near the camp and, one night, he brought her home a handful of seeds. She could barely sleep, waiting for dawn to come. She checks on them every day, but nothing has sprouted." She gazed at the camp around her, the light in her eyes dimming. "Nothing can grow here."

"Your turn," she said, and I threw a smooth stone, watching it bounce off the bucket's lip and drop into its center.

"Nice!" Sana exclaimed. "Ahmed suffered the most," she continued, lowering her voice and looking back into the tent at his still body under a tattered blanket.

"We had a cousin—Zain. He was five years older than Ahmed and Ahmed worshipped him." She smiled, shaking her head. "Dressing like him, talking like him, wanting to do everything he did. Zain was more like an older brother than a cousin, and Ahmed always wanted to be by his side.

"One afternoon, when they were on their way home from helping Baba at his shop, a gang opened fire on their bus." She stopped, picked up a stone, and hurled it at the bucket, almost tipping it with the impact.

"Zain was shot in the head,' she continued, "and Ahmed sat there, not moving, just holding Zain's hand. His body was covered in shrapnel and his face was splattered with his cousin's blood. He stayed like that until help arrived."

She picked up another stone and dusted it off. "He hasn't said a word since." She shook her head. "Well, as I said, only in his dreams. He can still hear the gunfire ringing in his ears."

"I'm sorry," I said.

"Me, too," Sana replied. "I was on my way home from the university where I was studying to be a journalist. When I arrived, my mother was hysterical and I had to piece together what had happened between her sobs. We collected my two younger sisters and left—without a single belonging—because we didn't want Ahmed to be alone a moment longer. We arranged to meet my father and Zain's family at the hospital, and after Ahmed was treated, we crammed ourselves into two taxis and traveled straight to the border."

I nodded. I knew what it was like.

"Well, that's not entirely true," she said. "Before we left our apartment, I did manage to grab something." She reached into her pocket and pulled out a piece of paper, carefully folded.

It was her high school baccalaureate.

"It's a reminder," she sighed, "that I have a future." She threw another stone, this one at last making it into the bucket. "A reminder of my dream to become a journalist, which can be pretty hard to hold on to … especially in a place where it feels like no one can hear you.

"You're lucky," she said then, and I looked at her, thinking that would be the very last word I'd use to describe myself.

"I heard your father talking to mine the other night. He said you have an aunt in Canada, and that your family applied for private sponsorship almost a year ago."

I nodded. It was true. Baba's sister, Eva, had studied

internationally at a place called McMaster University, and after graduating and receiving a job as a neonatal nurse at a children's hospital, she'd been able to apply for citizenship.

I had overheard the conversation between Baba and Mama late one night, after returning home from the embassy and pulling Moussa and me from the hole in the garden. Despite the increasing conflict, Mama couldn't imagine leaving Syria.

"How much time do we have, Lena," Baba had whispered, "until it is no longer their breathing bodies we are burying? We need to get the process started."

"You might not be here much longer," Sana said, her voice bringing me back into the present.

I shrugged, not really knowing what, if anything, it meant for us in this situation.

"What about you?" I asked.

"For now," she said, looking up to where a line of clothes, still dirty, was drying, "this is it. My little sisters can't swim, so my father refuses to cross the Mediterranean. We have no relatives in neighboring countries, let alone abroad. My parents' health wasn't the best to begin with, which is why my mother was at home, and these conditions—no proper food, water seeping from the top of the tent, the smell of urine ..." she shook her head, "... they haven't helped. We're not ideal candidates."

Wasn't it enough to be human? I wondered.

"Don't lose that paper," I said to her. And she smiled sadly, before carefully refolding and securing it back in her pocket.

An aid organization was recently set up in the camp and it gave jobs to Baba and Mama. Baba works in their clinic, alongside their team of doctors, and Mama, with her ability as a translator, was asked to be a teacher in the newly erected tent school. They've been able to make a small living, allowing Baba to buy food and supplies when he makes his weekly trip into the city. And sometimes, there's a bit extra that he puts toward things our neighbors need. I am too old to attend the school, so I act as a classroom helper, especially during math, where the students struggle the most. My job is to circulate and break down problems, check process work, and praise correct calculations.

"Today, I'm trying art therapy," Mama says to me, a small smile on her lips, as we walk to the school. She explains her lesson and details all of the donated materials that her students will use.

"Thank you for coming in early to help me set up," she says.

I look at her and smile. Slowly, life is returning to her eyes. She has taken great pride in teaching the students the curriculum, showing them ways to solve conflicts without violence. Through different activities and play, she's been helping them work through what they experienced during the war. I think that, in her eyes, every child is Moussa.

We approach the tent, plain white canvas stretched over a wooden frame, and enter through the front flap. The walls are decorated with the students' colorful drawings, and there is a large rug, with red and blue geometric shapes, spread on the ground.

This is where the students sit in a semi-circle around their teacher, who stands at the front, next to a pad of chart paper that has been tacked to the wall.

Mama sets out the paper, paint, and brushes, and I fill small plastic cups with the water we had left over from the large bottle that the organization provided. The students begin to filter in and I greet them with a smile. Mama moves into her regular routine, knowing how important this is for them. She welcomes them as they take their seat and then settles the group by leading them in the song, "Aatini al Nay wa Ghanni," by Fairuz, a favorite Arab artist.

"Give me the flute and sing, for singing is the secret of existence. And the sound of the flute remains, after the sound of existence ..."

As Mama finishes, I distribute the materials to the students, and they lie on their stomachs, propped up by their elbows, waiting for her instructions.

"I want you to close your eyes," Mama says in a soothing voice, "and imagine a place of safety. This may be a place you already know, or it may be one that you create, using your imagination. Now, I want you to turn to the person beside you and describe that place in as much detail as possible. What does it look like, sound like, smell like? And most importantly ... what does it feel like?"

Mama pauses as her students take turns doing this. "Now, using your brush, I want you to paint that space. When you're finished and they're dry, we'll put them up around the room; we'll surround ourselves with them. But remember, even though they hang here, you can always return to them—all you have to do is close your eyes." Mama smiles and the students begin to paint.

At first, there were few instructions about what to paint, but Mama found that the students would return to what they'd seen during the war, using their bright paints to draw dark images of tanks, of torture, of terror. Mama refused to let her students stay there, so she'd created activities that would guide them forward.

"Elias, you can head out," Mama says, gently laying the last painting to dry on the plastic table at the back of the tent. "If Baba's home, tell him I won't be much longer."

I nod and finish emptying the water cups before leaving.

"Elias!"

I am not two steps out of the tent when I hear my name being called. I turn to see Sana and Ahmed running toward me.

"Have you heard?" Sana says, a stricken look on her face.

"Heard what?" I ask, with a feeling of dread.

"There's a rumor the Lebanese army is coming to hand out eviction notices."

Ahmed's face crumples as his sister speaks.

"What do you mean?" I ask.

"They're going to level the camp," she says.

"But why?" I ask, thinking of what we'd left behind, of what we'd built. "Where will we go?"

"I need to find my father," she says, and she and Ahmed turn to run. "Tell your family," she shouts back over her shoulder, before disappearing down the next row of tents.

I run the rest of the way home and burst into our tent.

"Baba," I say, breathless. "I just ran into Sana and she said …" I stop, realizing that Baba is not alone. A fair-skinned woman with short brown hair and a navy suit stands beside him.

"Hi there. You must be Elias," she says, extending her hand to me. "I'm Christine, from the Canadian Embassy in Lebanon. I was just telling your father some good news."

I look at Baba, who smiles for the first time since he left for the market that fateful day back in Syria.

"Elias," he says. "Our sponsorship has been approved. Christine will be picking us up and taking us to the airport to leave for Canada, the day after tomorrow."

"But …" I say. "What about Ahmed and Sana, Mama's students, our neighbors?"

Christine looks at me sympathetically, and then turns to my father and shakes his hand. "We'll see you in a few days," she says, and nods at me before leaving.

"Baba, haven't you heard?" I try again. I'm almost hysterical.

Baba nods. "About the eviction? Yes, Elias, it's all our patients are talking about."

"I don't understand. Why would they do this?"

"It's complicated," he says, rubbing his tired eyes. "There are sanitary problems, security issues, fears of terrorists attempting to infiltrate from inside these very tents. Lebanon is a small country,

Elias. It can't permanently support this volume of people. But other countries are helping; we are lucky to have Canada."

"But how can we just leave?" I am shouting now. "What about the others?"

"It's a cruel lottery, my son," Baba replies. He shakes his head wearily. "When you're selected, you go. Everyone here understands that."

The next day the eviction notices arrive.

Mama opens ours and cries, placing a hand over her mouth. I know the uncertainty of her students' futures—their education, their lives—makes her feel helpless. It's like she's losing Moussa all over again.

I read the letter in disbelief. It states that refugees have two days to pack their belongings and leave the camp.

It names no place for them to go.

I grab the smooth stone that I keep next to my quilt on the floor, and run out of our tent and down the road to Ahmed and Sana's.

Sana is sitting outside, the eviction letter crumpled at her feet.

"A part of me hoped it was just a rumor," she says. She won't look at me as I sit in the dried mud beside her.

"I'm so sorry," I say. I wish I had better words. "Do your parents know what they'll do?"

"There is talk of an abandoned barn …" she cannot continue her sentence.

"How is Ahmed?"

"You know what?" she replies. "I actually thought he was on the verge of speaking. I felt, with your mother's help, that we might be weeks away from hearing a word from him. But this letter, and our parents' panic about it … they've forced him to retreat further into himself." She digs her fingers into the mud. "I don't know if he'll ever talk again."

"We're going to Canada," I say quietly.

Sana nods. "We knew it was just a matter of time," she says, and finally looks me in the eye. "We're going to miss you."

"I'm going to miss you both very much," I reply, and let the silence hang heavily between us. "I will look for your name in the bylines," I say at last, and she smiles at me sadly. "Will Ahmed see me?"

Sana shakes her head. "He won't get up from bed today."

"Will you give this to him?" I ask, pulling the stone from my pocket. "Tell him it is the one that always landed in the bucket."

Sana nods and we hug. When I reach my tent, I look back. She is still there, shaking the stone between her palms, as though it were a pair of dice.

We awake the next morning ready to go because, really, what is there to pack? We each leave with one item: Baba, his medical bag, Mama, her teacher's manual, and me, Moussa's drawing.

We begin to make our way through the crowd when suddenly I feel a small hand tug on my arm. I turn around and my heart lifts.

"Ahmed!" I am grateful to be seeing him this last time. "I'm so sorry," I say. I feel a mixture of anger and helplessness.

He wraps his arms around me in a hug. "Goodbye, Elias," Ahmed whispers. Then he disappears as quickly as he arrived, into a tattered crowd that has begun to leave the camp.

We meet Christine at the front of the settlement, where she is waiting beside a shiny black car that will take us to the airport. She is leaning against the passenger-side door, with the trunk open, waiting to assist us with our things. When she sees that we have none, her smile begins to fade but she manages to catch it.

"Peter, Lena, Elias," she says, when we are close enough to hear. "Are you ready to go?"

None of us answers.

"Yes," Baba finally replies, and she opens the back door for the three of us to slide in.

The air is cool and the leather soft under my skin, but there is no feeling of comfort.

We drive for several minutes in silence, up the dusty lane. I promised myself that I would not look back, but it's not that easy to move forward. With each glance out the window to my right, I crane my neck further back. Finally, I am staring out the rear window. I see the tents, blurred together and blowing in the wind like a white flag, begging for surrender. Above them on the hilltop, a row of yellow bulldozers, patiently waiting.

CHAPTER 14

CANADA

The morning sun breaks through Elias's bedroom window, a ray of light landing on Moussa's drawing that's pinned to his corkboard on the opposite wall.

As he lies in bed, Elias realizes that the colors aren't as vibrant as they used to be. He worries that, one day, his memories of his little brother won't be, either. He already thinks that the sound of Moussa's laugh—the laugh he tries to listen to on repeat—isn't quite right.

Turning onto his other side and rubbing the sleep from his eyes, Elias can hardly believe that he's been in Canada for almost a year. He thinks about how he'd never have made it through without the friendship of Sullivan and Liling, without the support of his teachers, and surprisingly, without soccer. Out on the field during practice one day, he'd looked up into the blue of the sky and realized that it stretched all the way to the field in Syria—and it made him feel secure, as though he were tethered to it.

Elias hears a knock at the door and rolls over to face it.

"Good morning, son," his father says, poking his head in.

"Good morning, Baba."

His father makes his way to the bed and sits down.

"How was your course?" Elias asks.

With the help of his sister, his father had been approved for a loan from the federal government that allowed him to upgrade his skills so that he could practice medicine here, in Canada. He has been renting a small room from a single mother in Hamilton, close to McMaster University, and he has been taking the bus home to Richmond Hill every weekend.

"It's challenging, Elias, but nothing we can't handle," his father replies with a wink, before pulling a folded envelope from his pocket.

"What's that?" Elias asks. Curiosity forces him to sit up.

"It's a letter from Nizar ... Sana and Ahmed's father."

Now Elias sits up straighter. In the chaos of leaving the camp, he didn't know whether his father had thought to give him their contact information.

"Are they okay? Does it say how Sana and Ahmed are?"

"Would you like me to read it to you?"

Elias nods and closes his eyes as his father begins.

"Dear Peter, Lena, and Elias,

"My sincerest apologies for not writing sooner. Our situation has not afforded a moment's rest, and I am ashamed to admit that I did not have the money for the stamp needed to send this to you. But during that

time, we thought of your family constantly. You were a candle in the dark night that was the refugee camp, bringing happiness to our days, and restoring our belief in the goodness of others. Even now, you remain a source of joy for our family, as we gather in the evenings and imagine your new life in Canada. We have given you many glorious adventures ... it helps us, thinking of what life should be. After you left, it was as if that candle were blown out, the light, our hope, extinguished.

"We left the camp the following morning, with no place to go, and no idea where to begin. The worst part was not having a plan to tell our children. Never before have I felt more of a failure as a father than in that moment, when I could not provide them with reassurance. I cannot think of a worse world for a child, than one where his parents do not know the answers.

"We spent the following days on the streets of Lebanon, begging for handouts from the residents who saw us as an infliction—or who did not see us at all. For three days, we consumed nothing but water and the smallest scraps of discarded bread. Finally, on the fourth day, when my wife and I were so weak that we could no longer stand, a man crouched down before me and said that he owned a small tanning factory, and that if we agreed to work for him, we could live there, too.

"It is from this forgotten place that I write you this letter. We were grateful to receive the opportunity, but cannot ignore the cruel conditions that we've found ourselves in. During the day, we work amidst the stench of decaying animal hides, and at night, we breathe in the fumes from the chemicals used to tan the leather.

"Sana soon developed a deep cough, and we made the decision to send her to Europe. She refused to leave without us but we forced her, telling her that her dreams would die if she didn't go. The journey was to take two to three days. Today is the fifth, and we have not yet received word …

"Our only wish now is for the war to end, so that we can return to our home and rebuild what is left of our lives. My wife and I worry that if we don't return soon, we will forever lose Ahmed's voice to silence, and his smile to tortured thoughts. We will always be grateful to Elias for returning our son to us, even for a short while.

"With deep regret, I have no return address to give, but will write again soon, with the hope of news to share. Please give my love to your family.

"Sincerely,

"Nizar"

Elias doesn't realize that he's crying until his father hands him a tissue to wipe away his tears. His time in the camp had felt like an eternity; he can't imagine what another year would have been like ... what creature another year would have turned him into.

But, for the first time since the war began, Elias does not feel like he's being acted upon; he feels in control. He stands up. Elias knows in his heart that one day he will go back to Syria. He will find a way to help those left behind. He will take advantage of the education he's getting in Canada. And he will use that knowledge to help his homeland. But for now, Elias has to be content with what he can do.

"Baba, can we speak to Eva's priest, Father Damian? Maybe we can see if there's any way Ahmed and his family can be added to the list of refugees that the congregation's willing to sponsor."

"I've already made us an appointment," his father replies, then stops Elias before he can hug him.

"There's no guarantee that the church will have enough money, or that the family will be eligible ..." he continues, then pauses. "But we must try, Elias. We always must try."

Elias embraces his father, and his father holds him tightly before letting go.

"Your mother needs our help in the garden," he says, then stands and ruffles Elias's hair. "Get dressed and we'll see you out there in a few minutes."

Elias closes his eyes and says a silent prayer for Ahmed and his family, before walking to his closet.

He grabs the navy blue and gold soccer hoodie that he's allowed to wear at school on Spirit Days, then tugs on a pair of old jeans. Then he makes his way downstairs and puts on his runners, before heading through the kitchen and out the patio doors.

Baba is on his knees, clearing out the roots of last year's plants, and Mama is standing beside him, talking to Liling and laughing, as she spreads fresh soil on the ground below.

"Hi, Elias," Liling says. "Your mom asked if I could drop by to give you guys a hand seeding the garden. I hope that's okay?"

"I'm glad you're here," he says, looking down to conceal from his parents the blush that is creeping into his cheeks. "What are we going to plant?" he asks his mother, scuffing the dirt beneath his foot.

"Whatever we want," she smiles at him. "Eva said the garden is our blank slate."

"I actually brought something," Liling says. Reaching into her right pocket, she pulls out three small bulbs, and then fishing into her left, removes one more.

"What are those?" Elias asks.

"They're jasmines ..." she says, slowly opening her hands so he can have a closer look.

"Today, Moussa, we are your favorite flower.... Yes, Syria's strong and sweet jasmine, and we are its seeds being planted ..." he hears his voice from a lifetime ago. *"And one day, when we see the sun shine again ... we will grow, blossom, and bring happiness to others."*

"I thought you could plant them here ... together," Liling says, reaching out to place the four bulbs in Elias's open palms.

Elias doesn't have the words to thank her, so he bends down

and, grabbing his mother's trowel, begins to dig.

He looks at the dark earth before him and remembers the hole in their garden back in Syria. The words, "Let's pretend ..."— the ones he'd always used to comfort Moussa and himself while hiding—come to his mind.

Elias pats the earth securely over the last and smallest bulb, stands, and brushes the dirt from his fingers. He turns and takes in the scene around him—his father, mother, and Liling laughing. The garden, like their life in Canada, will actually bloom. Elias realizes with a bitter sweetness, and for the first time, that pretending is something he no longer has to do.

ACKNOWLEDGEMENTS

I'm forever grateful to my publisher Red Deer Press, and my editor, Peter Carver, for providing a home for this important story and making my lifelong dream of publishing a novel come true. Peter, thank you for your expert guidance and support during this process. Your notes have helped me grow as a writer and have made my story leap off the page.

Thank you to my parents for giving me a deep and enduring love of reading and writing. Thank you for cultivating my imagination; I'll always be grateful for the maximum amount of picture books (forty!) that were borrowed from the library each week, and for the dinners that were delayed so the narrative in my make-believe world could continue. Thank you especially for planting the seeds of compassion and social justice within me. They have truly blossomed in my vocation, both as a teacher and a writer.

A heartfelt thank you to the Syrian community for its awe-inspiring bravery and resilience. I'd like to especially thank Kinan Bachour, Kamil Bachour, and Samia Al Rassi, for ensuring the authenticity of my story and its characters.

Thank you to my newcomer students whose courage, kindness,

and perseverance provided the inspiration for this story. A very special thanks to Maryam Jumaah, Parsa Vahabishekarloo, and Ma Sik Lun Ellen, for your incredible insight and thoughtful suggestions that informed early drafts. It's been an honor being your teacher.

I owe many thanks to Reccia Mandelcorn and the Aurora Public Library Writer's Group for their unwavering belief in my book from its birth to its final chapter. Thank you for your camaraderie and your invaluable feedback.

To my friends and colleagues, thank you for your endless encouragement and for sharing in the joy and excitement of this publication.

INTERVIEW WITH MEGHAN FERRARI

What made you want to tell this story?

Like many people around the world, I was shocked and saddened by the news and images of the civil war in Syria. Wanting to help, I felt that I might be able to make a difference through my teaching and writing. I hoped that my novel would raise awareness for those suffering, inspire readers to action, and create empathy for those new to the country.

What kind of research did you have to do to make sure you knew enough about the experiences of Elias and his family to make the story convincing?

I had to engage in extensive research to ensure that the story of Elias and his family was convincing.

This included reading news articles, analyzing reports such as the United Nations "Report of the Secretary-General on Children and Armed Conflict in the Syrian Arab Republic," and watching documentaries.

A great deal of my research was conducted through conversations with members of the Syrian community, as well as with my students, who experienced similar struggles in their native countries.

The novel shows Elias having to endure two kinds of struggle—first of all, surviving the lethal dangers of the Syrian conflict, and secondly the challenge in finding a place in the country his family flees to, Canada. Why was it important to you to tell of both these struggles?

It was important to me to include both of these struggles because, for many immigrants, these hardships go hand in hand.

A reader may wrongly assume that when people emigrate from a war-torn country, they leave their problems behind. The reality, however, is that they encounter a new set of challenges. For many newcomers, these challenges include issues of employment, housing, language, acculturation, mental health, and sadly, racism and discrimination. I wanted to present both of these struggles to provide the reader with a more holistic understanding of the newcomer experience.

I hope that by having Elias and his family endure two kinds of struggle, I was able to emphasize the strength of the human spirit and remind readers of the role we all play in helping one another.

Why do you think it's important for young readers in Canada and elsewhere to know about Elias's story?

As of 2018, the civil war in Syria has displaced over 5.6 million Syrians. Many of these individuals have taken refuge in Canada, with Prime Minister Justin Trudeau welcoming more than 25,000 in 2015, while others have settled in countries around the world.

I think it is important for young readers to know about Elias's story because they are likely to have students just like him in their classroom. I hope that his story allows them to better understand and in turn empathize with the newcomer experience. I believe Elias's story can act as a springboard into students' own narratives, as many share a story similar to his.

As an educator, I believe it is important for students to share these personal experiences, as this allows them to connect over common ground and lay a foundation where friendships can form.

Why did you decide to include the characters of Liling and Ms. Boselli in the story of Elias and his family?

Liling and Ms. Boselli truly exemplify the notion of Canada's being a cultural mosaic.

As an immigrant, Liling sees herself in Elias, and goes out of her way to make sure he feels both included and accepted. She is a testament to the many young people in today's world whose small acts of kindness are having a big impact on the lives of those around them.

Ms. Boselli's story is actually my father's story. I grew up listening to my grandfather recounting his experiences as a member of Italy's resistance during the Second World War, as well as his family's journey to Canada and their first few years in the country. The character of Ms. Boselli is an homage to the invaluable contributions that they and so many immigrants have made to Canadian society.

For you, this is a first novel. Often first-time authors choose to write from personal experience—from what they know. How did it happen that you chose to write a story that was not based on your personal experience? What would you say to young writers about the challenge of embarking on a project like writing a novel?

As an educator of English Language Learners, I have the privilege of working with newcomer students and their families. The inspiration for this book came from my students' stories of the hardships they endured in their native countries, as well as the challenges they faced as newcomers to Canada. I was inspired by their resilience, determination and perseverance, and their ability to overcome obstacles, while becoming leaders and role models in the community. In many ways, this novel is a tribute to them.

To young writers, I would say that embarking on a project like writing a novel is one of the most rewarding experiences that life has to offer. It requires a great deal of passion, dedication, hard work, and a desire to impact the world in a positive way.

I would recommend that young writers read as much as

possible, and hone their craft by taking writing classes in a variety of forms and styles. Additionally, I would advise young writers to join a writers' group that can offer support and aid in working through any challenges that might arise.

Lastly, as one might imagine, writing a novel is a tremendous learning experience, and requires a growth mindset. During times of frustration or setbacks, it is helpful to remember the words of Brazilian novelist Paulo Coelho: "It's the possibility of having a dream come true that makes life interesting."

Thank you, Meghan

Meghan Ferrari grew up in Caledon, Ontario. She received an Honours Bachelor of Arts in English and History and a Bachelor of Education from Queen's University, as well as a Masters Degree in Social Justice Education from the University of Toronto. She is an active member of the Aurora Public Library Writer's Group, and has published poetry and short stories. She presently shares her passion for literacy as an educator with the York Catholic District School Board. This is her first novel.